In the tradition of Italian film horror Argento and Sergio Martino, comes **A]
Doll**, a new hyper-surreal giallo from a Peter Marra (*Random Crucifixions, Peep-*

Two women in an unnamed metropolis. Two lost souls unchained and free-floating. They were unknown to each other until yesterday when fate forced their paths to cross. Two broken dolls on a perilous expedition to nowhere. They share three mutual desires: sex, addiction and murder.

These women are on a noir psychotic trip morphing into lurid Eastmancolor, speeding towards unknown pleasures, experiences and victims. These women don't care who is the target as long as their ravenous appetites are satiated.

Hands encased in shiny black leather destroy the night as unknown screams penetrate the atmosphere. A stiletto gleams in the moonlight. A straight razor silently performs its atrocious deeds. Children of sin lost in the shadows cry out in anguish. Blood drips silently onto asphalt. Your mind will twist and convulse under the avenging neon of the decaying city.

This is a tale about creatures from the underground. The people we never meet. The ones who are only whispered about.

These two cursed females are trapped in a barbed wire of sex, addiction and murderous violence, ensnaring both the innocent and the guilty. You'll cringe as the two femme fatales indulge their wildest fantasies as the body count grows. And you will feel their passion and rage, their guilt, and the torment of their original sin as their shadows follow you home.

A Naked Kiss from a Broken Doll will haunt you from the first caress to long after the final scream.

A Naked Kiss from a Broken Doll

by

Peter Marra

A Naked Kiss from a Broken Doll

For Polly and Brian

"The very fact that the commandment says, 'do not kill' makes us aware and convinced that we are descended from an unbroken chain of generations of assassins, for whom the love of murder was in their blood, as it is perhaps in ours."

Lo strano vizio della signora Wardh
(The Strange Vice of Mrs. Wardh)
1971, Directed by Sergio Martino

"Sexuality is the lyricism of the masses."
Charles Baudelaire

"The artist's experience lies so unbelievably close to the sexual, to its pain and its pleasure, that the two phenomena are really just different forms of one and the same longing and bliss."
Rainer Maria Rilke

"The behavior of a human being in sexual matters is often a prototype for the whole of his other modes of reaction in life."
Sigmund Freud
Sexuality and the Psychology of Love

Giallo

Giallo, meaning 'yellow', is the Italian term for crime fiction, named after the bright yellow colours of early mystery paperbacks. In Italy, 'un giallo' (plural 'gialli') can be of any nationality. But film audiences abroad adopted it as the name for a peculiarly Italian sub-genre of thriller cinema that had its heyday in the 1970s.

Although definitions vary, the giallo is most often characterised as an Italian crime film with murder-mystery elements. It often draws on a pool of common conventions: stylised murders, amateur sleuths, black gloves, repressed memories, enigmatic titles and creepy Ennio Morricone music scores.

Its parameters are vague, leaving plenty of examples sitting ambiguously on the fence between this and other genres. And it's a tradition that gleefully mixes high and low culture, where you'll find flashes of artistic brilliance sharing the screen with moments of jaw-dropping squalor.

~ The British Film Institute

A Naked Kiss from a Broken Doll

Inside the Dark Factory

The first corpse was found one week before. Reports indicated it was a male, about 50 years of age, who had a reputation for selling narcotics and engaging in stalking and raping. He was well-known on the streets by the moniker *Dirty Boy*.

The sex and age of his victims didn't matter, anybody would do and anywhere he could get away with it was fine. He was a loathsome slime that preyed on anyone, anytime, anyplace. The body had been discovered nailed to a church door. A thick spike was hammered through each wrist and likewise through each foot. According to the coroner, the killing occurred around 1 a.m. Saturday. The first person to discover the corpse was the sexton who arrived at her usual time of 5 a.m. Sunday, to prepare the altar for mass. Upon seeing the corpse dangling from the door, eyes open and blank, she vomited. In addition to the previously mentioned wounds, it was apparent that the throat had been slashed from ear to ear and the mouth had been given a Glasgow Grin à la the Black Dahlia. A coagulated pool of gore was on the brick sidewalk underneath the corpse. The door was splattered with a dried red color.

Deep red hallucinations.

Frisson in the belly.

Nightmare juice.

Before calling the police, the sexton took a slug or two of sacred wine from the tabernacle to steel her nerves. She tasted vomit and alcohol in her mouth, which did nothing to mask the aroma of blood and excrement permeating from the corpse. It required all her strength to dial the three digits necessary to summon the cops. After making the call and stating her emergency, she slid down to the pavement, facing away from the body and stared. She occupied herself with watching the starlings flit in and about the stone pines a few feet away. She started touching her fingertips together rapidly. She needed distractions.

The eternal caress of a blood droplet slowly cascaded from one petal to the other of the throbbing iris: tasting the everlasting arousal that this aktion inflicted upon her.

"Touch me here, insert the stem there," she whispered to a random figure. "I'll flog you when it's over."

The sound of leather on flesh was broadcast on local channels. Sparkle sparkle for us. She loved these things. It was a time for control.

Deleted Scenes

Lee Harvey Oswald hid in a movie theatre after the assassination; he was in the Texas Theatre watching *War Is Hell* starring Audie Murphy when he was arrested. Some say Oswald wasn't the assassin. Anyway, he was shot and killed by Ruby on November 24, 1963. The assassination might have been a sleight of hand, a special effect.

John Dillinger died July 22, 1934 in front of a movie theatre. He was betrayed by the Woman in Red after having watched *Manhattan Melodrama* at the Biograph Theatre in Chicago. Some say it wasn't Dillinger who had been killed but another poor bastard who happened to be in the wrong place at the wrong time. Maybe it was a last-minute switch at the crucial moment. Maybe John was saved by the kind of trick that only film can offer.

Charles Starkweather patterned his life after the movies, he studied James Dean incessantly and tried to dress, act, and walk like him. He invented the killing spree with his girlfriend, Carol Fugate, and he was killed in the electric chair June 25, 1959. It happened in Nebraska.

They came to the movies to lie in the projector's glow and hide in its arms forever. Their solace was the umbrella of comfort that only celluloid can offer. Their fevered brains were soothed by the cool hands of the Image.

Sometimes we open doors that we shouldn't be opening, and we walk through them as blind bastards. Other times we walk through them looking for a thrill, a brief shot of electricity to the soul.

The young girl sits at the kitchen table, not noticing that the neuron surrounding her home is stretched to the limit, but she senses something is wrong... Extremely wrong...

She likes the movies, but just for entertainment. She's only 11, thin and geeky, not knowing how things really are, not knowing the experiences of sex and death. She has had inklings of what these things are but he isn't exactly sure about it. She isn't certain if she is afraid or happy about this. She hasn't had the Jones for the movie narcotic but it will come soon. The sexual urge will follow. Soon she will take the shot of boiled down celluloid, the mother's milk, a shot that will send a fever to the brain and soothe her fears. Once it goes in it never comes out.

"Goddammitt!" the father screams as he takes a chair and smashes it and smashes it to the floor. The mother is upstairs yelling and nagging.

"Goddammitttt!"

The wood splinters dance in the air then settle to the floor. The girl keeps on doing her homework; if she keeps on doing his normal routine things will be okay. The Spelling assignment that she is working on requires her to make a story from the 10 words of the week.

"This will be a good story," she says to herself. "A story of deep red and purple things. Black and blue and what's in between."

The chair smashing goes on and the girl stops her homework, leaves the kitchen and enters the television room. She switches the TV on and watches and watches, drowning out the noise in the kitchen. The sound of the chair breaking, the sound of her mother screaming, drowned out as the loving hands of the cathode ray tube take her away.

It doesn't matter what's on the tube right now, just as long as there is movement on the screen. Every so often she glances towards the kitchen where the noise of splintering wood is continuing. It doesn't bother her anymore; the television is here. She watches the screen intently; the vampire on the screen is pale and thin lipped. She moves seamlessly through the fog and the darkness.

"She looks like I do when I have an asthma attack."

Suddenly the noise has stopped and a door slams, followed by a thud and some whimpering. The father is gone, went out for a walk, the daughter imagines. Maybe he'll come back and take her to the antique toy store tomorrow. They could talk to the proprietress, Aurora. She was very entertaining, and her collection of antique broken toys was fascinating to the young child. Some of the toys were made of iron, some of wood, no plastic.

Her mother is silent also. The only sound is from the television. Pale and wan, the girl watches and watches while shadows and images ricochet off the walls of her brain. She falls asleep in the chair briefly then wakes up. She goes up to bed, clutching her favorite toy — a troll doll with blonde hair. She knew it was lucky because branded on the figure's soles were horseshoes. She is not concerned. She is not bothering to see what happened to her mother nor wondering where her father went.

"I start here and it ends here. Then we can rewind."

She goes to bed and doesn't dream.

The neuron band gets tighter. The white noise gets brighter.

The demon crept in during the early morning. He was laughing softly to himself and he crept inside the girl, always chuckling softly so the child didn't hear. The trickster offered her images and solace; the child obeyed and rid herself of the pain.

Morning had come quietly and there was no sign of what had happened the night before. The girl walked around the house admiring the handiwork. The splintered chair was gone, the mother was gone and so was the father. Smiling broadly, she went to the refrigerator and took a box of Wheat Chex down from the pantry. She filled a bowl with the cereal, then added some milk, got a spoon and had breakfast. The young woman was calm and not afraid. She brought the cereal into the living room and switched on the television. She watched contentedly and ate her breakfast. When she was done eating, she left the bowl in the living room and went upstairs. The television was still on. She wouldn't come down for a while. The white noise grew brighter. Meanwhile, the grinning shadows she had left behind started to cry. They missed their daughter.

Experimental Animals

The musicians busking at the train station platform were driving her crazy. They were beating empty plastic pails that were once used to hold vinyl compound. Tribal sounds were ripping through the station, deadening the sounds of the subway trains. She looked around at the other customers to see if she was the only one bothered by the noise. Other people seemed to be grimacing, and she wondered why they didn't get organized and kill the drummers. They could jump them easily and throw them onto the tracks, right in front of the approaching train. She ground her teeth in silence. The deep hole in her stomach got bigger. It had started out as a small pinhole this morning but as the events of the day unfolded it grew and grew eventually morphing into the huge cavern that she felt at the moment.

When she first started this commute, the drummers didn't bother her, actually she once thought their drumming was entertaining. They put such effort into their work and their faces showed that they were enjoying the noise, the sweat, and the reactions of the crowd. She looked around and took another survey of the crowds. It seemed to her that almost everyone was enjoying the drumming now. Some younger people were actually slightly gyrating to the beat.

"It has to be me."

She thought of herself as an old punk rocker and she was annoyed by noise.

"I feel like such a fucking dick... an old and worn out fart."

She laughed to herself and continued waiting for the train. According to the announcements it would arrive in 7 minutes.

"Sid Vicious died for my sins."

Seven minutes came and went and the train still hadn't arrived. The platform was getting crowded with customers and the drummers were taking a rest, although the accordion music was still playing. The announcements were still playing: train arrivals for the opposite direction, opposite from where she wanted to go. Eventually the accordion music stopped, the old man was taking a break, the drummers were taking a break, and the crowd was still humming. She searched for the novel with the yellow cover she had been reading.

"Can't remember the name."

This was all she did lately: get up-take some vitamins-get dressed-go outside- buy the paper-do the crossword while waiting on the subway platform-go to work-work
go home-watch tv-maybe read, but not often-play on the computer-repeat as directed go go go.

This was the agenda for Monday to Friday. Weekends she went to see a movie. She stayed in the film embryo most of the weekend, by herself, always protected. She had finished the puzzle this morning, but she hadn't read much of the paper itself or looked at the movie ads.

She looked around and up and down the platform. Blank faces blank... blank. There was a smell of broiled meat probably emanating from the shish kebab vendors on the street above, sticky cooked flesh smoke and burnt blood drifting down through the gratings mingling with the smell of the customers. Every so often a rat appeared on the tracks. Bad sign: they didn't feel the vibration of any trains so they were more brazen walking up and down the tracks: there would be a long delay.

"I'm going upstairs, outside for awhile. *Fuck* me."

Pushing through the crowds she felt more and more annoyed, although she admonished herself since these things were out of her control. "Gotta relax. Please God help me."

She had taken to praying lately since she was always afraid. It gave her brief comfort. She kept on doing it several times a day because she hoped that eventually it would give her a great deal of comfort. She liked to Google prayer questions at night. All sorts of esoterica would appear: St. Expedite, Eleguua, Miracles, Prayers for the lottery. Voodoo. The outer regions of the internet made her happy. She curled up in its belly and clawed at the placenta.

She reached the stairway and slowly made her way upstairs. The man in front of her was grossly overweight and was moving slowly. "Fat fuck," she thought.

One step one step. She could feel the anger of the people behind her... as they watched the fat ass of the man make its way to the top. The anger floated in her belly but never made its presence known to the others.

Eventually the man reached the top, this meant she was free. She skirted around him and made it quickly to the other stairway which would lead her to the street...

She reached the street. She felt slightly better. It was about 7 p.m. now and she decided to go walk around. She had a need to take in the landscape and breathe the city air. She had exited near the famous ancient monuments.

Her plan was to follow the stations on the street, tracing her way home above ground, so when she got tired she could just duck into the nearest station and descend below the earth and watch the squirmy people and get home. She thought about many things on her walk.

The twisted noise that had been growing in her belly catapulted out of her stomach through her esophagus over her tongue and out her open mouth, it was preceded by a wail that she had never expelled before, a scream that seemed to last forever, but no one heard it, not one of the shadows noticed. She kept on walking. Then it happened again, expelled the form from her mouth and took shape in front of her. She looked around frantically. The creature, silvery and shadowy, translucent, looked at her with its huge round eyes and made a small noise. It seemed frightened. She couldn't make out its features, but it seemed to be a fusion of male/female sticky and beautiful, radiant in its own disguise. It froze for a moment then bolted into the night.

Criselda looked around quickly. There was no one on the street; she was in the oldest part of the city, not many residences around here. They were on a side street when it happened and the creature had bolted down an alley and disappeared.

Stopping under a streetlight, she stopped to get herself together. She was cold sweating, breathing fast, feeling faint. She couldn't think, her brain was melting panic-stricken. Her heart was racing, and it hurt. She saw a fountain and was grateful to duck her head under the running water.

"Let's rewind... Gotta calm down... fuck... fuck... me..."

She didn't know where that thing came from other than inside her, or why it decided to come out at this time, so she decided not to track it, not to try and find it. It had disappeared into the darkness of the city. "I hope I never find it. Let's rewind. My child... it's gone."

When she had sufficiently recovered, she continued her walk following the subway stations on her way to her apartment. She thought that she must be in shock since after the scare from the creature she had given birth to, she was experiencing a feeling of euphoria, of a giddiness which she couldn't explain. In a way she felt somewhat fulfilled as if she had accomplished something great. She should give that thing she birthed a name.

"When I get home, I'll look on the internet for some good baby names," she thought.

Behind her in the darkness of the evening, she heard a man screaming in pain.

"I hope my child isn't hurting anyone."

She was worried as mothers often are about their offspring, especially when they are in potentially dangerous situations. "Please God help it... Please God help it..."

A boy, about 13 years old, whizzed by her on a bicycle. He turned around and then stopped abruptly. He said words to her but her brain was racing and she didn't comprehend. His words were accusatory, but the tone of his voice was nonchalant, almost bored.

He looked at her blankly then hopped on his bike and took off. He sped up and passed by a rather large woman who was walking down the street. As he passed, she lifted her blouse up and exposed her huge udders to him. He looked once then burst into flames taking her with him. No screams, no noise, just a flicker as in a silent movie. After a few seconds only the shadows were left. Criselda walked over to the two outlines etched into the sidewalk cement and touched what looked like the woman's shadow with the toe of her boot. She waited a moment then continued on her way. The incident with the kid was very troubling. Criselda thought back to last week, trying to reconstruct the past, but she had no recollection of any even remotely similar events happening. But... it seemed to her that in the recesses, her memories were kicking around trying to get out that something had happened. Something very bad had happened.

Criselda strolled down the streets following the subways above ground. The moon was out and it was turning into a clear night. It was unusually warm, all that was needed was a light jacket or sweater.

She walked.

"How are you?"

She turned abruptly. A man was staring at her. He was slightly overweight.

"Okay, how are you?"

"Fair to middlin'. Fair to middlin'. Have to go to the clinic." She recognized him from the methadone clinic she passed by every morning. Although the clinic was unmarked, she knew by experience that it doled out methadone. The addicts would line up every morning and wait until the doors opened and the doses were handed out. She would see him outside the clinic chatting with his friends every time she passed in the morning. He was a very friendly man. He liked to talk to his fellow addicts, some hunks of hair and bone stitched together with time and spit. One of them always had a boom box with him playing the same tape over and over: "Fresh" by Kool and the Gang.

He was a nice guy. He had stopped to talk to her. She was grateful for the company.

"I have time to stop and chat," she thought.

"What are you doing around these parts?" he asked.

Unlike his fellow addicts at the clinic, he was a heavyset man about 30, with long graying hair which hung limply from his scalp and rested on his shoulders. He was using a cane because he was developing phlebitis from all his years of shooting up in his legs. The veins in his arms had collapsed long ago so he had turned to searching for new veins in his legs. Criselda knew this because about a month ago she had shared a subway ride with him, and he had decided to tell her his addiction story. He had covered a lot in the three stops that they were together on the train. He talked very fast.

"I'm on my way home. Where are you goin'?"

She didn't want to discuss how her evening was progressing. They were standing underneath a street lamp. The sodium glare was annoying her. She kept moving back away from the light so that he would step out of the yellow circle and get nearer to her to chat. She kept moving further and further backwards until they were in an alley behind a dumpster. He kept on with his droning chatter. She couldn't hear him. A few rats scampered away disturbing a puddle of water.

Her brain started squirming and the film started un-spooling. Instead of a rewind the fast forward took over faster and faster to its inevitable conclusion. The pain in her gums increased from the growth of her fangs her cuticles ached from the growth of her nails. The beast was out. Her friend didn't seem to notice what was happening. White noise... she saw his mouth move but no sound came out... fuzzzzz... the rays revolved in her eyes...

She lunged forward piercing his jugular with her newly grown fangs. Her teeth ached for release, they ached for something to destroy, the craving hit very hard. She got him in mid-sentence it didn't seem as if he knew what was going on. He looked at her with a sad startled expression. As he started to collapse under the shock and loss of blood she shoved her hand into his stomach ripping open the outer skin plunging deep into the stomach — it was warm sticky, and felt like a hot fuck — and brought it upward steadying him so she could continue her meal. The methadone or heroin that was already in his bloodstream started to make her dizzy. She had to rest. Slowly she lowered him down, laying him out. He was bleeding heavily.

"Why?" he gurgled. She remained silent and knelt down next to him. She ripped open his stomach and he let out a gasp, voided his bowels and he was dead. Criselda stopped. The retching started in her stomach and spiraled out of her mouth and nose. She splattered him and the ground with bile and blood.

She leaned back against a brick wall and wiped her mouth. She was cold and sweaty.

"I don't know..." she replied.

The alley was painted red, black and yellow. She stared at his body for a while, not knowing what to do, half expecting him to start his conversation up again.

She remembered when she was a child how she used to make snow angels in her backyard. She liked the sound of the snow as it gently fell, the sound of the snow would block out her thoughts, it was a slow gentle sound that dusted her face as she lay down, looked up at the gray sky and moved her legs and arms. Then she would carefully get up and look at what she had created. She would do this many times during the day. If it was a snow day and she was home from school, it was even more special.

"That was before this..."

She eventually walked out of the alley and looked up and down the street. No one was around. She was dressed in black: black boots, black turtleneck, black leather jacket, black jeans, so she didn't have to worry about the blood showing. She continued her walk home following the subway path. She walked unsteadily at first. The slight intoxication she had received from the blood/narcotic was still with her, but as she walked, she could feel herself sobering up, yet she felt somewhat nostalgic for the high, as minor as it was. This could be dangerous. Criselda shook off any memories of that type of recreation. She was walking more steadily now. Her legs hurt and her eyes were wet. She wanted to lie down in the snow somewhere far away and make a few angels. You hurt me so much dad.

As she strode, she noticed a spider crawling beside her. "Hello beautiful," she said to the spider. The spider didn't smile because they can't.

"I have to speak to you," it said.

"Oh?"

"You can't keep up like this. You can't keep going like this. I'm your conscience. You aren't doing nice things. You're doing very very bad things. I was sent here to guide you and to offer you salvation. I'll stay with you from now on and protect you, make sure you do the right thing."

"Oh, that would be great. That's so nice of you," Criselda said.

At that moment Criselda stepped on the spider and ground it into the ground. The crunchy-crunch was very satisfying. She felt as if she had accomplished something today. The spider said nothing when it met death. He was flat and he was not moving.

"Maybe you'll come back as something else, something more pleasing, maybe a snow angel, maybe a nice thing, maybe a circus clown, no don't do that, clowns scare me."

She started to regret what she had done, since it was only trying to help.

"Someone always tries to help and I always spit in its face."

"I'm glad you feel that way maybe there is hope for you"

She turned around and the spider's ghost was hovering in the air before her.

"You can't lose me. I said I was sent to help you. I see this will be a difficult job."

Criselda saw that a subway station was ahead. She walked quickly, the spider-ghost floating behind her. She tasted her fingers trying to get high of the junkie's blood that was still on her fingertips.

"Maybe I can suck it off my sweater and get a quick jag."

She ran down the station steps quickly took out her fare card and pushed through the turnstile. The train was just pulling into the station. The doors opened, the bell rang, and she was though the steel doors. The spider was gone. She sat down. There was only one other person in the car — a homeless man asleep at the far end of the car. The whole car smelled like shit. She sat down and rested.

The black dog is after me. She made it up the stairs. The squeaky creatures peered thru the banister at her as she made her way slowly, slowly up the stairs. The front door closed slowly behind her, so slowly in fact that she worried that someone may have snuck in behind. She turned around ignoring her audience at the banister and walked down the stairs to the front door. She pulled on it hard — it was locked. She turned and again made her way up the stairs. The squeaky creatures snickered at her. At the door of her apartment she stopped and retrieved her keys. Once the door was open, she stuck her hand inside and felt for the wall switch. The light flickered on and she stepped into her apartment, into the kitchen. It was the same, nothing had changed. It was just like she left it this morning. The walls were still flecked with blood. There was a pool of blood on the floor. The blood was about 15 hours old now, so it was well into coagulation. Good thing it was winter, or there would be flies. The blood smelled tangy and full. She smiled to herself and walked into the dining room, being careful not to step into the puddle. Her life was so full of blood lately, she thought to herself. This stuff and my clothes are caked with it — the blood and smack of that junky who was always so nice to me I shouldn't have done that, I shouldn't have done this. Why can't it get better, why do I feel it why the white noise the crackle the masturbating idiot sound I always hear in there. The subway drummers will start again soon. The final clump clump darrump bumpo that throb that robot voice next train in 2 minutes the following train will be in 6 minutes and the times were never right anyway tap-dancing Chinese man all sweaty smell death she... she went back to the kitchen and stuck her index finger gently into the puddle... a ripple in the pool also gentle... Oh so gently it tastes like pain and salt... he suffered a long time I made him beg and then I finished him... they always pay...and I always make them beg... are you listening daddy... ??

The spider's ghost, feeling despondent, left her alone. It knew when to mind its own business.

She went into the dining room and stared at the mirror (the full length one, her favorite one). Her offspring stared back. Life was good. The curtains were closing; the spider was smiling and floating gently.

A Crucifix for Forbidden Pleasures

When Criselda awoke at 3:35 a.m., she became aware of a remnant from the previous night's activities. She savored the delicate taste of blood in her mouth. This flavor lay on top of her tongue like a wilted iris, soft, cloying and sinister. How this happened, she couldn't recall, but her taste buds tingled. She really wasn't concerned.

Hot channels were throbbing in the back of her throat, slightly burning as the sensations snaked their way to her stomach. It always happened this way, so early in the morning, in that dead time they call the Hour of the Wolf. Luminous fluid was refracting the light off her own skin. For a moment the sound of blood rushing though her veins startled her, then she grew accustomed to it. Multiple exposures made her unhappy. Her thoughts came quickly. Now she tasted iron in her mouth. That thing was happening again. Another life arrived as tortured bones and dust. She whipped every part of her mind until the sounds became sobs.

Each glazed look she received punctured the cat's eyes. Criselda was in pain. The pain was behind the eyes, needles piercing light. She killed the sounds for her own sake. The removal of its heart last night had turned into a sexual conflict.

The suspended embryo watched us all through the cage of crimson glass.

[She spoke to the Neon last evening. "As one of my lost lovers used to say, 'I wish things were like they once were.' So, we can erase the inappropriate circumstances. If that makes you happier, I need to do it."]

She was puzzled when he said last night, "I remember dominance—a terrifying experience—and I remember a typical eye-brain loop... Abstract to the eye. Kiss me. *Unh!* What did you do? This hurts so much. I loved you. Why? I know someone is there. I know someone is here. The steel hurts."

Sounds of metal slicing flesh, getting her revenge, she couldn't control her giggling, bloodstained fingers trying to hide her mouth. They mustn't see this.

Criselda smirked at the memory of him twitching in a red pool on the floor of his luxurious apartment and the satisfaction she felt when she pulled the blade out. Low moans of pleasure. The click of the switchblade closing and the way it felt, the heft of it in her black leather gloved hands made all the aggravation of stalking and executing him special. Worthwhile.

Rapid repeated strokes of throbbing stiletto switchblades. Repeat as necessary until all used up. Prescription for lust. She thrived on these sounds. She lived for the found effects. As Her eyes glowed in the purple evening through her veiled face, we could see a glistening tear. She frequently indulged in special effects in the Cinerama of shattered desires. Inside the dark factory, personalities were dumped to make room for more pain. She craved the immediacy of the defoliated scenes.

In the next street she saw broken woman parts in the shop window, fragments of a prior personality never to be pieced together again. Parts shared to generate new personalities. Mama mama please birth me a new identity. Papa papa please hide me in the basement; my hobby will be the defenestration of Daddy. Then, bodies will kiss the random faces as they float gently downwards, just like leaves in autumn.

She thought in images variously vacillating from torture to serenity to lust. Vibrant blue eyes watched her intently. Blue Eyes turned to ebony when the entry had been made. What do you want from me? They ran into the womb of the black leather evening. They fucked for three days in pools of warmth that mutated to red. Cold concrete cool stone for inspiration She hid in between the holes in the darkness.

She was aware of two ongoing incidents: the soil shivered slightly under her bare feet and the flesh had become soft.

Example 1: she used her tongue to trace infinite semicircles under the eyelids and paused to flick lightly over the lips protruding through leather. These lips trembled ever so slowly. A sound of wincing caused a shiver [right there]. This thing: the removal of auditory impulses and satisfactions. Razor dreams and deleted scenes: the metropolis was heaving, but no one else noticed. The tone was upsetting, the images were always black and white. It's bleak, but it should move faster. It was her impressive signature example of intrigues and deceits. She marked her territory with a switchblade and blood. Carving sigils here and there. Example 2: she was setting a strong rhythm now. "What do you see, when you see yourself?"

She was sensing a stronger rhythm now. She sensed the Black Glove again, twisting inside her. It was numbing her nervous system so she would not feel guilty about performing depraved acts. These rapid-fire images slid off her brain and were tacked to the wall. The nude state of her neglected ego caused many distractions. It was the christening of her open heart. Sequestered emotions.

"To please me, the camera eyes will weep," she said.

She saw the burning women pleasuring themselves. They were echoing faint sighs of the lost animals on the beach that was near to the city. A conversion from dull to sexy was repeating itself. She fought the grip of the traveling vines of morality. Now she saw its eyes. *Her* eyes. There was a body being laid out on the kitchen table. It was surrounded by white napkins cradling razors and scalpels. She signaled for the beginning of the dissection. Her lips were dry — she licked them. Her labia were wet — she caressed them. She had indulged chronic self-fondling all day long, just to get herself in the mood.

(flash-bang)

Back and forth feeding frenzy. Her exorcist lived in a dark factory, pumping blood and political views; she knelt on the floor and created images of pain. This tasted lovely. The air was bitter with smoke and iron. Beneath the foundation of influence was discovered a wayward woman. Her hobbies consisted of instigating crucifixions and attending public humiliations. Mama. Mama, please take me to Confession.

Papa. Papa please believe me, they lied. I didn't do all those things. They lied. Pain for the second father figure complex. Drums were slashed behind the curtain behind her. Behind them, secret rituals of flesh were conducted. In between the cobblestones appeared rivulets of urine speckled with blood. Yellow canvas red dots. Sooner or later the forensic team would be called in. Love is the basis of all nature; love is the basis of all snares. The women kept their slaves in the cellar where they served as healing nourishment for their mistresses. The clock that hung upside down spun backwards every 13 hours. It made no noise. Inside the frame was an action portrait of a woman pleasuring herself. She was turned on by the tortures of the forgotten. Memories of regrets ate the souls of the wanton figures. Tales of lustful deceit made her whole again.

"What have you done to her?"

"It's an indication that the saints should always kill, my sweet-baby... my sweet-baby!"

Take that life and screw it up. Jet black magick. Feed it to her... the fossilized remnants of porno loops projected always in the back of her brain. She told us everything, she just spilled her guts.

"And then I emasculated them, there were throbbing cocks in the curb by the basilica," she continued, swallowing saliva with great difficulty, "you know, they were remnants of past transgressions. A handful of experiments that went wrong."

She decided to practice witchcraft in the dyed yellow dying evening. They told her she felt sexy. She gazed. She gazed. She was being displayed for gratification. Descendant character self-description as the second-born claimed new victims. It had become a Black Sunday for her laughing children. Tight and throbbing Thanatos had infected her. On the steps [at 11 pm] she was sitting in front of Basilica Sant Agostino. The struggles of the deceived made her smile. It was 84 degrees Fahrenheit outside. She drank from a paper cup that had been re-used several times. It was always filled but she never discovered what the liquid was — the mysteries of transubstantiation bored her.

Exactly 100 feet away, in front of her, the musicians spasmed and passed on. It was an alchemist's fuck, it was a witch's feast. There was a death in the convent that she had heard about. This interested her. She lay back on the steps and gazed at the blank black sky. Optically aging and arguing, oozing through a labyrinth, doubling once more upon itself, consummating the unseen sexuality riding the night's ashes. The reflection was primordially sexual in nature She stalked her prey and made plans. An archetypal Jeanne d'Arc, a re-born Beatrice Cenci. She attended the opening drama of the well-bred housewives who were boring in their simplicity. Dresses pulled tight and ripped off. Rubbing their skin with a new batch of Flying Ointment, communing with the nature that detested all of them. She knew they were lubricating their cunts so the drug would enter the bloodstream quickly. Fast tract to salvation. The misfortunes of leading a virtuous life dogged them. Scientific twisted faces of destruction had become the norm. Obverse of the temple, ritualistic slayings, wilted red roses in abandoned pale churches. Fleeing fingers ran from disembodied faces. Beneath the Pantheon female silhouettes grasped at cool marble and clung to cold mouths moistening their eyes at the realization of a lack of love. So much guilt and so much pleasure. Their hair was ebony with faint traces of crimson. Long strands flew away in the recent nuclear breeze, collapsing walls of wide-open eyes. She listened intently to exquisite songs of loss. These symptoms eviscerated her attraction and betrayed her denials. Seeing their pain made it easier.

The restless desperation of her cunt destroyed the timepieces she had collected because an absent timeline always appeared to her. Since she was trapped in a room, she decided to make the best of it. Black leather hands fondled an open razor. After confirming that her victim was gagged, she slashed where appropriate, making sure the blood was histrionic.

She shivered, she moaned, mimicking her victim's orgasmic death throes. When the spirit had left the body, she repeated her aktions and reaped the rewards. The figure twisted off the crucifix. Later, she exited and gingerly navigated cobblestone streets balancing precariously on 4-inch stilettos. Turning right into an alley, she paused and studied her clothes under a streetlight: a few red streaks on her clear vinyl raincoat. She studied her face in a compact mirror she had withdrawn from her purse. An additional two streaks of gore on her left cheek. She wiped herself down and exited the alley.

Tomorrow morning the corpses would be discovered. Maybe. Or maybe when the flies started to murmur. Back at home, in her small studio, she inserted a dead mourning dove into her cunt. Tears streaked the dirty window. The sacrament had been completed. As soon as 3 a.m. arrived, she searched through her bookshelf and located a school yearbook. She drew targets on the faces of the nuns who had taught her in parochial school.

A murdered time. Struggling with her. Police suspect in her mouth, she had covered up, but now she stripped under black planets. Call of a rare victim. Wielding a knife while wearing the raincoat. Deep in the background landscape. Sliding into the foreground landscape. Visiting the locked door. Short moans caused shame. She usually moaned loudly in the presence of a stabbing. A vulva descended from a sky that was devoid of color. A teardrop of crystal, razor-sharp in its deception. Duplicity excited her.

She perused the morgue photos that she had stolen last night and tossed on the bed. Revenge cleansed her. Hide and seek. Detect a human order of things.

"I felt a strange calm as if some enjoyment was near."

Was it the result of excessive hallucinations at the hands of the goddesses? The blood crept slowly up the crumbling political monuments. Eyes glinted at the monks that were licking the marble fingers in the garden. A sound of a whip for the scream of feminine loss.

"I'll be waiting for you once it's over," she had said.

A bloody veil drifted to the floor. Forgotten models of civilization. Teeth will protect her as she wanders. The tribades will devour the gifts.

She confided, "I used to fuck 'em in the abandoned nuclear bunker. It was a few years ago. Crappy distant memory of exquisite pleasures truncated by religion. They were always watching us, but they paid us. It's okay I guess."

La Maison Dieu card tossed on a pile, she grabbed it and held it between her breasts and smiled.

Mostly populated with indecent strippers coated with paint, International Klein Blue 79 (IKB 79).

"I couldn't wash it off. I watched as the wife licked Salome's legs, working upwards to the sweet spot. Later to enter the cervix. It's a state of addiction. One upon a time there was a happy couple pounded with nails hanging by the clocks that throbbed with blood. Incessant ticking. Spastic licks and nibbles. Dripped right onto the faces below. They were so loved. So wistful and penetrated."

The fake priest unexpectedly reached out and grabbed her ass. It was the last lascivious act he would perform. The sound of a saw cutting though live bone always aroused her. A new wetness dripped down from his cuts and from her crotch, puddling onto the black marble floor. She adored the sounds of stiletto heels on stone.

A Mannequin's Bloodstained Fingers on a Naked Model

The day of reckoning, after so many postponements, had arrived. She observed that it was like the creative process, this destructive process. It all depended on her outlook and how she should channel the destruction into a new memento. The offal was removed, washed and securely stored away in a Lock & Lock and placed in the refrigerator. She wiped her hands on her polka dot apron. Time for a torture garden.
It's a state of addiction.

She always smirked after receiving the menacing phone calls. She fled into to the alley and licked her fingers. Always trembling, she frequently looked over her shoulder, left then right. Left then right. The pattern never changed. It was time to resurrect the pornographic hallucinations that comforted her. Clad in corset and restraints she was the dominatrix and submissive simultaneously. She strangled her lovers with the leash and placed corpses in the veils of vibrating shadows. Kneeling before vacant symbols she renounced all that she believed in.

The relation of the Cimabue Crucifix to herself: each glazed look became part of the film collection that she guarded jealously. She was happier after she removed the narrative sense. She cringed when she saw the damage done to the cross. She noticed paint chips corroded by benzene as they floated by her knees.

Criselda started losing a grasp on time. She usually prevented her victims from whispering. She tried to abort their yens. Trembling and sweaty, she sat down in the cool puddle for relief. This caused her ebony pupils to dilate, emphasizing the bloodshot characteristics of her eyes as the soothing fluids caressed her pussy. The cobblestones felt cool on her ass. Utilizing severe closeup, the camera lenses traveled the route of the red rivulets coursing through the throbbing plane of white. Pupils dilated, orbs frantically moving back and forth side to side in a spastic cum. She masturbated for full effect and relaxation. The effect would show up nicely on the screen, she decided. Once the camera pulled back everyone would understand through the overhead shot. What could she do now?

"I know someone is there. I know someone is here. The scissor hurts."

Some memories can be unnerving, causing a twisted cold feeling to take root in the pit of one's stomach, pressing on the spine and wrenching the heart. They're usually followed by palpitations and cold sweats.

Other memories, the pleasant kind, can be used as a sedative to placate our fears.

A long time ago Criselda discovered beauty. As a reclusive adolescent she often stayed home many Saturday evenings watching Creature Features and Chiller Theater. In New York City the local stations often broadcast horror and science fiction films on Friday and Saturday night. *Alphaville* must have been part of a generic sci-fi package purchased by the station. No one had bothered to check the plot — futuristic — cold, high contrast artful, dark and French. Criselda was engrossed by the film and attentively watched, then *she* appeared on the screen, she was clad in a dark cloth coat trimmed with brilliant white fur. Criselda's eyes brimmed with tears, as she realized that she was in the presence of the personification of Eros and style. The actress's sly smile comforted and thrilled Criselda. Criselda got up and sat in front of the television. She traced the woman's face with her right index finger, leaving an outline of moisture on the screen.

Coffined thoughts and luscious lips were pressed against the obverse of a guillotine. She had discovered a new way to bisect the labyrinth and eradicate the home.

As a teenager she bolted to take refuge with fellow addicts, nymphomaniacs and criminals. Criselda was always burning with a fever that destroyed and created. This was a murderous phoenix always on the prowl and never caught since she was always reborn. Criselda decided a long time ago to inhabit the barren landscape and feed her brain on the lurid, obscene and sanctified. She would obliterate the victimizers and relish desolation. She fed on the bleeding and the splatter. She was to avenge the victims, taking out the persecutors both submissive and dominant, manipulators all.

"I couldn't continue living in safety and wholesomeness, I was poisoned and vilified. I imagined that they were dead. I had to kill it. I had to kill them."

A step towards the Master Death first ever recording of the effects of a superb vagina. The ramifications of an interaction with a spoiled bitch holding a detached morbid penis between its legs. Dangling down at the 6:30 position. She had indulged in the portable frenzies of thrashing pleasures. No relief.

Criselda greeted each day by re-doing her plans for a destruction of the play motel.

She would sneak into room 217 and find out what the resident was keeping in her top bureau drawer. There was water running in the shower, audible behind the closed bathroom door. With her gloved hands, Criselda slowly pulled the drawer open and quietly rummaged through the contents. She found a black corset that was barely new, two pairs of full fashion silk stockings with a French heel, a riding crop and a rather large black dildo. Criselda took the envelope she had brought with her labeled "my filthiest thoughts about you," and left it on top of the hosiery. She smiled and gently pushed the drawer back into the bureau, then exited the room as quietly as possible. Her upper lip was coated with a thin layer of perspiration and she felt rather light-headed. Luckily, she could make it back to her room, number 117.

She lay down on the double bed because she felt slightly feverish, caressing her knives for comfort. She felt safe now. Numb go numb now. A knife tears the self-portrait asunder. Shards of canvas dot the night sky. She went to sleep. Too nervous to attempt the second orgasm. Stimulation reduced the agony.

Her satiny channels glowed, and time became chance.

Unquenchable Thirsts

A strange vice in a garden of incredible lust situated where the television no longer dwells. Remnants of a photometer measuring thin slices of numbers that were tattooed on her lower back. Always the photographer's model. Always chased. Never chaste. A television had been inserted into her heart so she could endure the orgasms of the industrial age.

Part 1 was painful, drawing her body in. Part nine made her wet. Parts 2 through eight caused her to see a purpose. Just a phenomenon. White noise returned as the feminine leather figure clad in an electric corset strolled through a garden of earthly delights. 1, 2, 3, 4, 5…

Watch the trailer. It details the cause of her disappearance. It outlines the tales of disgrace. The rigor mortis of the saints screamed in the back room. "I'm sure you'll like it here. Hear me please listen. Kiss my whispers. The saints always hide the corpses. They're used later in obscene films of a political nature financed by the government and the religious institutions. Everyone knows that insects are telepathic. You are too. You saw the Holy Ones before they arrived."

She entered the hallway of slow cries. Her flesh was crimson. The sonatas had finished a long time ago. Behind glass doors, in low light, opiated ecdysiasts masturbated their customers with knives. Each client held a flashlight to illuminate the dance of female fingers on cocks (also to make sure they weren't robbed). She looked behind them at the plaster wall that had a fresco of an unending sentence of short words that described her horrific deeds. The audience remained in their seats kissed by curare, injected with guilt.

One dancer made the sign of the cross 70 X 7 times. Just like they said she should. This dancer was clothed in a skintight black satin corset that held up silk stockings flecked with red.

Criselda admired the contrast of the satin against pale white flesh, while a spastic flute droned on, fluids were milked.

"I pull on the chains, but I can't leave," the stripper said. "If I had no chains I would still stay here. Torturing. I know someone in there. I know someone in there. The scissors hurt."

The iron taste in her mouth was comforting to Criselda. Her labia quivered. The narrators will change. It was necessary. Reverberations of her lust. That was what was described to her, so she laughed because it was expected.

"I see a confessional," Criselda said to someone not there. "It's burning to the ground under the left-handed moon that's always watching. It sees. Cover her mouth with the ashes so she can rest a bit. She can start up again."

It was 10:59 pm. She rested on the steps leading to the Basilica of Sant'Agostino. The cold marble was comfortable. She drank fluid from a paper cup that had been used many times. A transient lens panned, starting at her feet, caressing her body and capturing her face, solitary and pale. Across the piazza, a plasticized vampire captured faces of transient creatures. The whirring undertone was slightly unnerving. A Madonna di Loreto cracked incandescent lightbulbs with her teeth, holding shards in between her lips, shaking with the aftermath of a good orgasm. It was the kind of cum that one feels for several minutes afterwards. The type that carries an afterglow born out of warm water. The pilgrim's Madonna flayed the skin off Caravaggio and constructed a fashionable purse. This figure sat on the steps and counted hours until sunrise. It had hollow eyes and she drank unknown secretions from a reusable lunar eclipse. They had become a passing fancy of de-frocked priests who were shivering under the cloak of Catholicism.

"Do you practice Magick?

"Can you sleep now?"

(Eviscerations of the de-frocked priests; an unspoken tale of the feminine supernatural.)

Hidden in the decaying architecture the numerous insects communicated with one another. The pastor noticed that this activity caused much consternation among the congregants especially during the act of transubstantiation when there was an escalation of the pain threshold. The sermon used only nouns and pronouns which added to the discomfort. Verbs and adjectives were strictly forbidden. Vague modes of communication were encouraged.

It was just a shadow of what the idea had originally been. It was just a bare sketch of the murder that had occurred.

"You must keep attending mass, that is the only way your black soul will be saved," a congregant had told Criselda.

After the service, the pastor was buried under the altar. No marker of his existence was found. Three years later, at midnight, the body was exhumed. The congregants made a solution from his remains and mainlined the liquid at the 13th stroke of the clock. They particularly liked the blood-blossom in the syringe barrel on the pullback of the plunger. A hymn for Saint Blaise was sung. On the nod. Not too much vomiting.

"You can go now. Take any mode of transport."

The room was composed of glass walls with an iron floor. Within the room were 3 plexiglass dividers. Here and there were rust spots caused by blood clots, a remnant of previous visitors. She kept writhing female mannequins attached to each divider. They had become a forced audience for the pornographic. S&M soliloquies were viewed hourly on the 127-centimeter flat screen television mounted on the back wall. Constant monitoring. Criselda was frustrated that the audience was devoid of sound. Plaster actresses fucked plastic actors. Pay one price. Manipulations of cunts and cocks were performed to the accompaniment of perforated brass disks inserted into antique music boxes. She had to crank them up when the spring was entirely unfurled. Moving quickly from 1 box to another, the task was quite difficult.

Gentle vulvae.

A placid woman rode a bicycle down a European street, red hair caressed by an August breeze. Intermittent sigils were left on cobblestones. She remembered that the music had never been transcribed. A transformation occurred — she craved other things now. The addiction had become furious.

They adored the taste of steel and leather after a hard-used fuck (atonal moaning of perversities). Her cold hands removed a previously colder heart — a glint of rage reminded her always of those things. A shine of a razor was titillating. The blade made delicate slices in the dark blue satin corset (the stockings were still attached).

"I need more tranquilizers now, no more colors; monochrome lives forever. I needed..."

Plastic Figures and Unknown Confessions

Criselda had no recollection of being born in this country. The black leather gloves felt snug and comforting. Her hands were secure. She made a tight fist and inserted it slowly. The aromas of tender flesh and sweat mingled with the gasps of the recipient, who with furrowed brow and eyes bleeding, arched her hips higher at each thrust. Periodically, their pleasurable moans pierced the evening. The body was left to rest and be baptized in the claw-footed tub in the corner. Criselda departed wearing sunglasses, a black leather trench coat and the remnants of a smile between her legs. Her stomach was clenched and empty. Some nourishment was required. She cringed when memories mingled, gorgeous debris melded into a soft construction of deep blue irises, petals trembling. Synthetic impressions fading.

A room lined with skin was in the back of the basement. It was here that the interrogation began.

"Do these photographs mean anything to you?"

"I was awakened by a nightmare," she replied.

"Be patient, your accomplice is being vivisected in the back. She had the hair of the deceased in her possession."

"I carry the victims' ivory cameos in my Chanel purse. Take them out and fondle them sometimes. Her face was so smooth — untouched porcelain, I wanted to lick it. Visceral. So, I murdered her during the political ad, the one that usually runs before the milk commercial. She was so turned on, such a willing fuck. I really stretched her out. See, when I had my hand in her cunt, she had her brain in mine."

"She was panting, her eyes swirled, and her face and tits were coated with sweat. I loved her so. What have you done to her?"

"This is where we hear confession." Nuns slapped Criselda's face hard. She peed herself. The others giggled. "I needed..."

Myrrh teased her nostrils.

Female, pouty, long-toothed beast with cravings. Clad in sweat, black gauze and red corpuscles, she pushed her ebony hair away from her face. She sported the latest hairstyle because it gave her purpose. The wind pulsated.

She held a lit red candle in the shaky fingers of her left hand, bent over slowly so they could savor the action, bent over slowly so she could savor their reaction. Her fingers caressed the waxen dildo.

The moans had been discovered by her pale blonde gamine in the adjacent field. This was the friend who was enamored of licking tombstones.

(glass spheres crack under heat.)

Make sure they are shut up forever. Disjointed ramblings get her off. They were undetected by the wireless cams. Their tongues vibrated in unison, a community of mutual homicides. Criselda bent over slowly. She was still holding the red candle; wax had started to drip on her pubic mound. She reached from behind and slowly inserted the candle deep in her cunt. In this way the candle illuminated the magick lantern slides. Each slide depicted the image of a mammal in ecstasy. Each slide contained a backdrop of assassinations (some of lovers, some of icons).

After the services had concluded, the participants sat cross-legged and told obscene stories that had been handed down from the ancestors. Fingers were licked. The Le Jugement, Le Pendu, and L'Hermite tarot cards were inserted deep into multiple willing cervixes. The music of Serge Gainsbourg and Jane Birkin was provided by way of vinyl recordings and stereo equipment. The brides dripped. The grooms had died. They had been brought home so they could serve a purpose. However, they had a different direction in mind. In the drive-ins some murders occurred quite often. Blood stained film clips documented the revenge of the American Housewife. Sometimes we slipped away to hide from the American way of life, but it always caught up with us. We retrieved many words and obtained much pain.

She was discovered nodding out in a chair in a random room. We don't sleep naturally, only narcotics give us solace. Only pills give us dreams. There was a puddle of semen and blood on the floor. Turquoise lips with onyx screams latched onto her quivering breasts. She suckled the invaders until the walls cracked. She ran from cops in trench coats while bats murmured words meant only for her.

"Why do you obey these creatures?" Criselda asked. She lifted the doves that had landed at her feet. The white birds quivered due to slit throats. She gently kissed the wounds. Criselda's eyes teared and her pussy drooled. A voice was passed from one to the other, each owning it for only several seconds. Incurable lust was incubated.

"Don't you think your analysis was too severe?"

Saint Sebastian experienced ecstasy as each arrow reached its target, the writhing membranes stretched to epiphany. She remembered the scene where the female victim was on her knees, being flogged by a mistress. Tactile leather sounds. Both women were dressed in Roman garb; the supplicant's dress became increasingly fragmented and bloodstained as the cat o' nine tails bit into the fabric and subsequently her flesh. Bloodstained shreds of sheer fabric floated gently to the floor, punctuated by crescendos of moans and sighs of unexplained climaxes. The embryonic pleasure journeyed into a full-blown crash.

The peeping Tom was eviscerated, his eyes removed. The body was suspended from a balcony. The dripping blood anointed the passers-by, unaware of the gift they were receiving: a baptism into a new religion of automobiles and used-up humans.

"She was a friend of yours, wasn't she?"

Criselda had been transformed into the amorous purveyor of dark deeds, her hands encased in black leather, her fingers relishing the dead animal flesh that encased them. She adored the smell of vaginal fluids on her gloves. The aroma of the blood from the gouged-out eyes lubricated her sex. The screams became embedded in the hissing clouds, hidden in the abandoned villa. Their lost names were inscribed on its stone foundation.

The colors of red and black had a special significance for her. Torso enflamed.

She approached the crowd and was confronted with willowy apparitions. Shadow tongues licked her face gently. Slender faces repeatedly looked at her, sizing up the competition. One shaking hand grabbed her by the throat and pulled her inside. She was held in a twister of liquid and lust. Criselda lashed out, then on second thought, held them close. Faint murmurs, then passionate screams, finally morphing into petite morts as fingers removed eyes taken for sacred uses. Leather hands caressed silken flesh as blood mixed with mud. What you see on the screen is a Rorschach test performed by the last victim, a cadaver for the golden shadow wrapped tight in a black satin corset.

Torsos became screaming bodies stretching their sexual organs for maximum satisfaction. They had escaped from the Cathexis Clinic and were starting to spasm violently since the medication had been stopped. Discarded IVs lay on the ground, their contents leaching into the soil. As a result, foliage resembling crocuses sprung up. Spring was coming soon.

Unclassifiable noises.

Virgins appeared and started to harvest the budding plants.

Later, she will crucify the police informer after she stalks the remaining sacred visages of flexible demons. At home now. She rested on the black velvet couch decorated with the faces of Our Lady of Sorrow and Madonna di Loreto.

Outside, the cobblestones leached the odor of rain and held her alternate faces captive. So jealous of her possessions. The filthy aura of the room was pierced by stilettos. The phallic heels penetrated her as she indulged her leather passion while gazing at reverse pinups that ridiculed her.

"You're going to have to listen to me now. You must belong to me and no one else. Our love was written in the blood of the savior centuries ago. I'll call for help, they'll be here soon. The parts will be replaced then we'll merge once again."

Her eyes peered at us from under the crimson veil. She could see herself standing next to me. Slowly flaying my skin. The burn of flesh removal achieved new ecstatic heights for Criselda.

"Scream for me, it excites me so much." Criselda said.

A flash of steel shredded the evening. Feminine footsteps, deliberate, punctured a silence. Leather on stone, muffling the song of despair.

"Please give it back to me. I want what's mine. It was taken from me by force," she said. "The sign of the cross was executed 3 times. We'll hide here until the killers leave. (No one knew, it was familiar)."

The voyeur had claimed Criselda's sins.

Paralyzed hands were in formation. It was time to execute the patriots. Good night, it's time. She lay on a bed of crushed light bulbs and dreamed for 7 days. Ballads had been written about previous assaults. Pain had been ignored.

Broken Magick Street Girls

The telephone was out of order — no signal. We're alone now. They're waiting for me. They know my sins. They're dancing with a corpse.

Malediction from her lips caused the leaves to tremble and her parents to die.

After shuffling tarot cards with her saliva-coated hands, she raped the television and annihilated all transmissions. In the cemetery, the mannequins wore latex or leather and entertained themselves by second-guessing serial killers. Criselda longed for the ambient vampires who told her the truths. She longed for the company they provided as she hammered nails into coffins of photographs. Each photo depicted a dead relative.

By the ocean, other creatures waited for her. In the movie house, her costume was ripped off and she began to increase her cathexis. This felt correct.

The humid air was wrapped around her head, increasing the throbbing. The epitaph read, "I'll make you suffer."

Crimson lights throbbed from behind broken windows. Criselda decided to speak.

"Everything you are about to see and hear is based on actual events and witness testimony. All artifacts have been destroyed. As the years passed, the lovers consumed one another. I had my reasons."

"One evening, one fainted and the other sliced him open. They were stitched together and later set on fire. Many death masks were replicated and sold in the bar. There was an enchanting display on a table next to the jukebox."

The violence of hallucinations caused her to fuck anyone again. Generating a trap.

The violence of hallucinations caused her to fuck herself again violently with discarded flowers from the abandoned exhibitions, where love had once dwelled. They are gone now hiding in bombed out bars and disillusioned houses of torment, where happy families once dwelled. Random slices of thoughts littered the highways. Cosmic Go-Go dancers and goddesses maligned by the populace escaped from morality and smiled at the murders.

A classic courtesan tongued the gibbous moon, then wrung it dry. She inserted it deep into her cervix for new explorations in pleasure. Criselda tongued the moonlight as she draped erect cocks with rhinestone necklaces, to be inserted later into her cervix. Vibrations caused her nipples and pubic region to tingle as she achieved morbid climax after morbid climax in a short time-space.

The audience applauded before they were embalmed in vivo. She collected sweat and blood, flinging it in their faces. Invisible impotent authors, the architects of the degradation, were flayed.

"Your cock is so sweet; the mouth never lies. The moths die now. Your sex has the odor of roasted orchids, the nostrils are consumed. Tactile pleasures lead to theoretical climaxes and the lights of the cars double-exposed and delineated a buxom silhouette before the fatal crash."

Many tongues. Many fingers. Curled hot iron twisted between her wet legs. The movie posters were torn down. The strippers had left for the day. The stage was vacant. Hollow eyes behind the backdrop the hookers were likely to construct a new religion that was more honest and open.

"Come on darlin'. That's it. On my face! That's what was requested for salvation." She escaped unharmed in the bent light.

A miscellaneous prostitute wandered randomly in pursuit of her purpose into an apartment on the 7th floor. Perhaps she had the wrong address.

"Who's there?"

In the living room the chalk-lines moaned and moved slightly. This scared her.

click click click

The blade tapped gently against the grimy windowpane. Looking through an outline of a figure whose eyes were gouged out, she decided to imitate and plucked out both her eyes. This would please her parents. They would know what happened to her. The searing pain in the back of her neck was caused by the straight razor invading the cervical plexus, slicing nerves C_1, C_2 and C_3. Blood spurted out onto the brilliant yellow wall, etching her name into the plaster. Her eyes looked upward as an iron rod was inserted into her vagina, pushed through, travelled along the alimentary canal and exited through her mouth. Spit Roasted. The rod was inserted into a huge cement planter that had contained soil, no foliage. She had become an adornment. She had become a piece of furniture. Pendulous breasts were on fire. Her arms started twitching and urine watered the soil. Her purple satin corset was stained with red thick fluid, edging the tops of her full fashion stockings with the Cuban heel. Fungus grew in praise of the killer's achievement. The murderer fled through the missing door.

"Please identify the other ones. If it's not too much trouble."

The coroner (aka her pimp) said, "It was a curious fact that there was minimal fluid on her bare ass. Red ligature marks encircled her throat and occurred post-mortem. She was one of the prettiest women I had seen. With an abnormal shape of pain and a slight emphasis on pleasure she had fucked her way to completion. They pushed away from her, a dildo about 7 inches in length was shoved in her cunt. Never cared much for tragedies. Can I leave now?"

Incandescent letters shimmering, throbbing, rose from the steamy ocean. The sky as background was slashed in several places. Bloodshot eyes peered through the slits. The sky as plastic backdrop quivered with each stroke. Re-arranged, the 8-meter-high letters spelled out "BIRTH OF CRISELDA" in Broadway font. Amphibious beings leapt out and descended. Cellophane coated with shellac caught on fire. The projector lens crackled but continued. The silence was a backbeat.

Police scanner inappropriate music inordinate touching under radio waves. Blatant rip-offs. Politically correct fucking. Self-righteous deserved diseased crucifixion deaths. "I'm sure they'll love it! So clean! So pure!"

Voiceover: "Yes? The telephone is dead... I guess I loved him. I was... ashamed, so I removed the eyes. He wouldn't see what I had done to his lovers' victims. You can't keep pushing it in. The splatter only activated my guilt. I had that taste in my mouth again, my teeth vibrated softly. This music... the sounds in the sacristy... two depraved beings plotted more depravities... words of confession. I slowed it down then shoved it in deep, deep, deeply... lovely..."

Criselda paused, she was unsure where to go with this. She wiped her forehead with a white scarf retrieved from her coat pocket. She then wrapped the white silk around her neck, making sure to knot it fashionably.

"I came as he died. The Rorschach I made from his semen puddle told me the perpetrator's name as I climaxed once more. This was my pornographic augury. It was a gentle cum. Barely noticeable. A cat was shivering in the far-right corner under the crackling glass... Unfortunately, the killer was almost untouchable... After a few moments I retrieved the cere-brospinal fluid (a shock absorber for the central nervous system) and cooked up a shot. The liquid flashed up my vein and punched into my brain. It became difficult to speak as the new beings that sprouted up gave me a list of things that I had to do. His time was finished in the night of the clocks. They're waiting outside for me, but they will receive false love instead and then you will quench their thirst."

"This is my child. Don't take it. You can't."

She had many lovers and she described all her fascinating perversions to them. She had many victims and she described all the fascinating perversions to them. The fabric had been torn open to reveal overripe breasts, this lewd canvas was ripped open to reveal scenes from an embryo interrupted in development. Beyond that was a view of her mother and father's faces in twisted boredom. A new death, an old birth, a baptism of sulfur and ice. Leave before you can't. Head for the subway to the next borough. Out. Out. Her lives had become false interiors. Lush and lovely women beckoned. White turtleneck sleeveless she ejaculated many participants, remotely holding them deep until they were all dead. They gasped for air under the floating mattress. Satisfaction sublime. Fine and lean she leaned against the bathroom sink and filed her nails. Flecks of blood on her bosom made her laugh. She toyed with the black ligature and dragged them along the floor. Three episodes of sexy: it was what she had craved for so long Her love was tested. She kept its presence as she nuzzled Lupa Capitolina licking its moist nose and suckling ever so quietly.

Voyeuristic Tendencies

Criselda began the next day with loving gestures. She tongued the detached head, twirled the veins with her tongue, made a cocktail of vaginal fluid, urine and wine. The essence of femininity. She gulped it down to relive the junk-sickness. The petals of the impending afternoon lay at her feet. She didn't remember painting her toenails metallic Klein Blue. IKB 191. Criselda stared at them for a few moments longer. Her portrait should be done as another Fire Painting, she mused. Time to go.

There was a crescent in the corpse's left hand. Based on the progression of rigor mortis, she had been dead about 8 hours. Criselda kicked its foot. Pretty stiff. Criselda fondled the vial of holy water she always carried in her left pocket. The corpse was lying face up, her eyes protruded though the zippered eyelids of the leather mask. Her tongue lolled out of the zippered mouth. Another fetish death. A red silk ligature was knotted around her neck. Aside from the mask and the red silk, the corpse was nude. Her fingernails and toenails were painted a familiar shade of blue. There was a long smooth slit, as if made by a razor or scalpel, that ran from the navel to the crotch. Maybe something had been removed. Forensics would be required to collect specimens. Criselda closed her eyes tightly. Fire paintings of naked French models paraded under her eyelids.

[Later the perpetrator got into their car and admired the blood splattered dashboard. Murder Scene #1. Always admire style.]

Transcript of 911 call: "I feel so sleazy and incomplete nothing satisfies or removes these voids that make up my personalities the lights went out. Somebody switched them off. I'll use the razor again and the neon will throb. Wasteful time. There are 2 people. Help me please. I'm in the apartment don't leave me alone but I won't tell. I know everything the other one has done. I promise I won't tell. No. The steel heals me. Red vinyl stilettos in the warmth of summer. Rain cloaks her, but she's not hidden she sees me always. She tells me what to do. No. The wounds are raw in a mask of tears. Just some vacant old memoires. Don't really amount to much." She held a handkerchief full of obscene notions and kissed them, wiping her face with the rag.

The red painting on the wall was created by employing various methods of applying the paint. To begin, an assortment of different rollers was used; then later, sponges. This had created a series of varied surfaces. In this case the medium was not paint but human plasma. The image on the floor had been created by dragging a nude female still alive coated with gore across the white oak floor. Studied measures of guiding through the pain. The female was murdered offsite. Nothing could be allowed to destroy the artwork.

"I finally felt like commenting on it. Before that, I had nothing to say."

Their eyes were open. Their mouths were clenched. They were mass-produced commercial objects. Criselda knew their plastic language. The words that hurt. He had remained and kissed her forehead. Her lips quivered, then became calm; theoretically caressed but never touched. She sent him away so her mute characters could be counted. Criselda resisted but leather hands led her outside, a varied array of monochrome voices begged her to perform a random action again.

[Criselda felt sleazy and incomplete, nothing satisfied or removed the voids that clung. The voids that at one time composed her personalities. The lights went out, an unknown figure switched them off. Razors refreshed, glowing in the neon. There are 2 new people (help me please)...]

The current state of her life had become static. Criselda detested it. Every morning she woke up with a slow fall starting in the center of her brain and dropping down to her stomach. Some mornings, it was paralyzing. Some mornings she broke out in a cold sweat. She decided more deception was needed. Or maybe more discretion, since she was often criticized for hiding her feelings or being to blatant. One feminine fingernail drawn blithely upon the shadow, delicately creating a sexual slit that wisps of ideas might pass through.

"And you believe this? An unfortunate percentage of murderers walk freely, sequestered among our friends, relatives and lovers. Clothed in human skin draped over passionate animalistic cravings."

Criselda recalled that she had been buried alive at one point in her childhood. Buried once, twice, over and over. Jet planes crashed in random countries. A sky was tinted pale green with specks of white. She could feel the life being removed. Twisted, then bent out of shape. Ebony stones re-cast under the ever-present evil eye.

As she walked away, she glanced occasionally at the faces that her feet tread upon. Absent tongues licked cold stiletto heels, defining new origins and tableaux of fetishism.

"Do what, go where? Buona notte. A nice woman, elegant. Classy, but secretly depraved. There's a hint of a violent sadistic streak."

During her walk, Criselda decide to pause and conduct an experiment in humiliation. It was fortunate that she was wearing a skirt with no panties. She adored the feeling of the balmy breeze on her pussy in the evening. She found a face in the glass that looked up adoringly. Its mouth was open. She crouched down and pushed the fluid through her urethra. Precious golden liquid cascaded into the receiver's craving mouth. Hungrily, it gulped down the urine. Its eyes rolled back in ecstasy. Criselda smiled and giggled. She was happy that no passers-by noticed. Without wiping, she stood up, pulled down her skirt and went on her way. She admired the shop windows, stopping in front of a shop with plaster casts of female heads in the window. Criselda observed that her pubic hair was still damp. She reached though her skirt from the top and slid a couple of fingers inside her labia.

Criselda opened the door and entered her apartment. The lights were out, a pale moonbeam danced across the oaken floor. She threw her keys in the bowl that was on top of the old French bookcase with glass doors that stood by the door, then flicked the light switch. In the furthest right corner was a huddled mass of flesh that moaned slightly. It was naked, female and sweaty, about 40 years old, slight build, generous bosom. Criselda walked over, grabbed the woman's hair and yanked her head back. Criselda brought her lips very close to the woman's left ear.

"Who the hell are you?" Criselda said.

"Please leave me alone, don't hurt me... I need..."

"If you want to be left alone, why did you break in? Why are you sitting in my home, sweating and yelping?!"

"I had nowhere else to go!"

"Who are you?!"

"I... am... am... I?"

Criselda let her hair go, the figure crawled closer to the corner and attempted to roll herself into an even tighter ball than before. Outside the leather windows, several ravens had taken roost. Criselda was getting a little nervous and decided to sit down in the ripped recliner she had found in a dumpster a few weeks ago. It was covered in black leather which felt comfortable against her bare legs. After a few minutes, Criselda walked over to the woman and started to inspect her body. No injuries, however, when Criselda separated the woman's buttocks, she noticed that a circle of words was tattooed around her anus. The tattoo spiraled as a corkscrew. The anus had the delicate beauty of a purple blossom and quivered slightly when Criselda gently blew air upon it. The tattoo read: *"laissez-moi à mon hiver de cuir, à mon souterrain trava"* — "leave me to my winter of leather, my underground work." Criselda recognized it as a quote from Tristan Tzara. The ravens outside were starting to peck on the leather windows. Criselda banged on the windows and they departed quickly, the rustle of their feathers soothed both women. Criselda smiled.

"So...what do you call yourself, what's your name?"

"Cenci."

"Like Beatrice?"

No answer was forthcoming. Criselda sighed. She thought about how she loved the visceral mortal pleasures of this world. She loved the human form, male and female, if they were attractive. As she looked at Cenci, it was all Criselda could do to stop herself from sticking her tongue into the woman's anus and dragging her tongue out and around in gentle circular motions. The tongue would trace every tattooed letter around her little octopus's mouth. She would follow that by sucking the hole gently, adding copious amounts of saliva. She was certain that the anus would shoot out electric sparks that Criselda would capture with her tongue, roll around in her mouth, and shoot into the lady's ebony haired pussy. The electric jolts would mix with the aromatic ooze that inflamed Criselda's nostrils. She would interrupt these actions occasionally to kiss the lovely rounded buttocks.

Criselda started to feel feverish and faint, so she decided to force her thoughts elsewhere. Meanwhile, Cenci, who had been quiet for the past 10 minutes while Criselda had turned inside herself, started to shiver. Criselda noticed the slight twinge.

"Would you like something to wear?"

"Yes please."

Criselda got up and went to the bedroom. She returned with an old flannel robe that her parents had gotten her for Christmas 10 years ago. She helped Cenci into the robe. Criselda noticed how cold Cenci's skin felt. The woman tied the belt on the robe snugly and turned to face Criselda. Criselda detected a faint smile.

Cenci had performed in pornographic films a few years ago. "Just for money," she would often say, but she had admitted to herself that she enjoyed it. She liked being a dominatrix most of the time, but sometimes she got off on being a slave. In either case she liked the idea of something possibly going wrong. Either the bondage would be too tight or the slap would be too hard or the razor blade would cut too deeply. Anyway, things had always been safe. No headlines here.

She knew Caravaggio's tongue painted with shadows and his fingers were tipped with crimson. Cenci pulled his mouth closer, deep inside her, wrapping her legs around his sweaty neck. There was a brief pain, then she grew rigid, finally relaxing and flooding his face. Her arousal permeated the atmosphere, achieving aching colors that went beyond the spectrum.

"Solstice," Cenci said. "My love is a labyrinth; I've collected my knives and straight razors. It will happen soon. A cat is ripping and tearing near the pineal gland. It's clicking/clacking — fired up. I'll take those violators with me. They thought when I was in that room I wouldn't leave. I'll erase them in the maze. Dead eyes created in my image. Vapid smile, yeah, dead eyes. They stuck a lot of things in me, lubricated me so they could go deeper. It was the wrong shoot. In the back of my mind I knew it, but they forced me. I could have left. I could have left."

Criselda was shaking. Cenci continued.

"I was gazing at the ceiling. Admiring the intricate runways through the cracked plaster. Various colors streaming from eyes. My fountain of youth. They kept going. I couldn't wash it away. The stains are tattooed on me. I couldn't take anymore fuckin'. No."

Cenci showed the stains to Criselda. Criselda registered no emotion. Cenci's flesh was unblemished.

"It is nothing that I can assign a touchstone to," Criselda said.

Blasphemies and Bloodstained Fingers

The women left the apartment. They walked the absent streets. It was 1 a.m. The streetlamps were stretched out far and wide reaching up to the roofs of the buildings. This gratified Cenci, but disoriented Criselda. The overlay of the sodium lamps frightened her, but she could exert a modicum of control on these unfurling fears in her stomach. Criselda was almost weightless now, she glided along. She would be floating if she didn't stop, but she didn't care.

The pinpoints betrayed her source of enjoyment. One more jab for relaxation. The holes in the skin betrayed her empowerment. Her eyes were pinned. Redemption by syringe. Criselda was an expert in benign neglect. She ran with a pack of quiet animals, eventually turning on them, eventually slaughtering them all. She had some bones hidden in her rooms for good luck. Her fingers trembled; her lips quivered whenever she thought of these deeds. She wanted to go to the movies, a double feature would be nice. Something pre-1980. Maybe commit some crimes, maybe she would see some crimes being committed. This would reinforce her theory on the decline of civilization. She had no sense of God, although she had loved God in the past. No touching please.

There was no sense of history in New York City.

"That's why I left," said Criselda. "I need antiquity. Where did these flowers come from? Have they no gifts for me? Their silence hurts me. Pinpoints. Pinpricks."

Laughter could be heard from behind leather windows.

Criselda gingerly placed the device on the table. She selected the playlist and started a tune playing. Her visitor struggled to speak and to move several times, but he was unsuccessful. The more he moved the deeper the leather tongs cut into his skin, forcing blood out that started to trickle to the floor. The chair that he was bound to creaked, Criselda liked the noise. His face went pale when Criselda flicked open the 12-inch switchblade. Hazy vision of steel glinting through his teary eyes. Slowly, she dragged the blade across his left cheek.

Laughter could be heard from behind leather windows.

"Do you like the song?" she said. Slowly, she dragged the blade across his right cheek.

You'd watch my heart burst then you'd step in
I had to know so I asked...
You just had to laugh...

She sang along in a very low voice, making thin slices along the way. She would take her time. Criselda considered just flaying and getting a complete face that she could hang from the living room chandelier. His quarters were opulent, he was obviously rich. Why did he commit those crimes? His victims, all female, had died horribly slow, bloody deaths. The victims were either in their twenties or over seventy, twenty in all. The police had long been baffled; they hadn't tried hard enough. A hunter captures a hunter.

The blade moved slowly around the perimeter of his face, peeling the skin away, a quantity of blood trickled. "Must sting," Criselda thought.

"Does it hurt, baby?" The ball gag muffled sounds and his saliva was dripping.

"Don't worry about peeing, I tied a leather shoelace around your cock. I bet it feels numb. Your penis is rather small by the way... might take it with me and show my friends."

His eyes glowed with hatred, pure and throbbing. She was content. She removed her leather skirt to display her seamed stockings with the French heel and ran her fingers through her pubic hair.

"I know you have some fetishes, especially related to a woman's legs. Do you like this?"

He looked to the left.

She stopped peeling his face and drew the blade across each cheek alternating directions making crisscrosses. The blood flow piqued her interest. She dragged a leather gloved hand across his forehead. The perspiration stained the black leather. The wetness made her slightly dizzy.

"I'm just starting," she whispered into his right ear. She then proceeded to lick his face slowly. The blood was mildly salty and piquant.

"So pretty, so pretty."

He didn't have much leeway in his attempts to avoid the blade.

"You know why this is happening, you remember what you did. Do you see us now?"

Criselda was glad that he lived in an apartment with all the conveniences: refrigerator, stove, oven, etc. She went to the freezer and retrieved some ice cubes. Giggling, she dropped them down the front of his shirt.

"Don't pass out now, baby. You must be fully awake."

She grabbed the leather thong around his penis and testicles and pulled it tighter. "I'm just getting started…"

A solitary black bird at the window was waiting for something. Orgone accumulated behind its eyes.

Amid the cooing of the chanteuse slight sound of blade slicing flesh. Slowly, slowly.

She decided to continue with the extraction of the face. He

gurgled in a barely noticeable way. When done Criselda held the face up to the light. Her hands trembled as she peered through each eyehole. Before going into shock, he could see her looking through what had once been his face.

She anticipated the elation she would have when she extracted his still beating heart. She had to rest for a few minutes. Criselda sat down with her back to the wall facing him. He had fainted but he was still breathing. She was happy; she had more work to do. She knew she would climax at the exact moment when the heart would be lifted from the chest cavity. Aorta dripping...

Criselda stood up and walked over to the depraved creature. She pulled out a scalpel with a long strong blade from inside her leather café jacket. Without hesitation she plunged the blade into his chest and with difficulty sliced through flesh and cracked bone around the heart, forming a lid that she removed. The heart throbbed, Criselda started to perspire as a wave went through her, resulting in an orgasm, once, then again and again.

Caravaggio often flew into murderous rages, resulting in one known homicide. Hot fresh blood. It was suspected that the lead content of his paint had leeched into his brain, causing his social abnormalities. The colors flowed through his system. A purity of purpose.

Corpuscles are infected; when this occurs, they have been observed to dance. Oftentimes they move in twisted paths. The light touch of her kiss will send them scurrying. The veins throbbed and sweltered. Baked. Criselda felt the absence of empathy again.

Fingers clutched her skin on the way down. Lifeless eyes bathed in vacant light.

"There is no truth here, you know? I'm going to destroy their faces, their bodies, rip them apart."

Unknown Confessions... and Broken Mirrors

Criselda decided to fabricate a plot of fear. String it up by the old bridge that lead to Wonderland. 1:30 am the screaming would start. The cloying sounds would fill the auditorium and saliva would stain the floor. Juice will drop down feminine legs, blood too, from a constant state of arousal. The climax never ended. Two figures writhed on the floor fighting for the fallen stilettos; high heels pierced the remains of the evening.

Please maintain a veneer of respectability. Fucked memories, a souvenir of killings done properly. Shimmering liquid under the moon. Lick it off the blades. Lick it all then pass the Red into my mouth. I have bad ideas in my head. Surf music scorched rubber gasoline perfume mixed with female arousal odors behind the garage on West 3rd. That woman loved it in every hole, she liked to tell her girlfriends all about it. Then, when she was spent she would reinvent and vivisect her lovers. So much garbage. Hopefully they would stay alive during the procedure. It made Criselda giggle.

At this moment she was in the confessional. Purple words flowed freely, as she fingered between her legs, rubbing the clitoris. A taste of holy water and the smell of frankincense and myrrh. She saw a string of flickering lights from the ninety-nine-cent store. A string of lights that had been used to strangle previous customers that had entered the booth before her. They had never left. She moaned excitedly then left leaving behind a bad confession. Not knowing what else to do, she opened a vein in each arm. Penitents who passed by stepped over the red pool gathering outside the door.

In the park, mutations of former trees bore mute testimony to her slowly gathering fear. Acid-nerves-twist in the pit of her stomach. Minutes ticked by.

"Only I identified Death. It's easy," Cenci said while removing a cigarette from a beat-up pack. She and Criselda were sitting on a couch in Criselda's apartment.

Cenci lit the cigarette and dragged the smoke deep into her lungs as she was lighting it, a feat that always made Criselda gag. Didn't matter, Criselda had quit smoking 5 years ago, enjoying a piece of nicotine gum now and then. She would chew it in private since she was self-conscious about her chewing.

"The dance of cadavers as they fucked on coffins," she continued. "I saw them. Yes. Juice stained the oak lids." She stamped out the butt after a few more drags. "Didn't want it anyway," she said. She reached under Criselda's skirt. Criselda wanted to push the hand away but relented and let Cenci proceed.

Sightless eyes watched them as they indulged, the air was permeated with the smell of sex and skin and cigarette smoke. The pitch-black pubic hair was on display, matted into a sopping mop of fear and cravings. A scorpion twitched in the corner. Criselda reciprocated and parted the lips to catch a fleeting glimpse of the Oracle. Later Cenci posed for photographs in the bedroom while figurines were placed on discarded organs.

Bent over, Cenci's heaving breasts swayed with the rhythm of Criselda's hand plunging deep into her vagina.

"Please! Please! Go deep! Cenci begged. "It's been so long. I killed the last one! Aaagh!"

Black fire radiated from Cenci's pubic mound, turning into radiant crimson, enveloping Criselda's fist. Screams started and stopped and continued for seven minutes. Criselda's screams, then Cenci's moans, then together, lips touching, they collapsed on the floor, having rolled off the bed.

"You okay?" they asked each other simultaneously. Neither answered and they lay on the floor nauseous and tingling, staring at the ceiling. Three hours had passed. They looked for the clocks, but the timepieces had been removed. Having entered a maze, they had become entrapped.

13th Hour.

Criselda noticed that the nude woman had a tattoo on her chest, right on top of the breasts. She couldn't perceive it clearly since the woman was rather far away. As the woman got closer, as her mouth got closer, Criselda could see that the image was an animation of Christ on the cross, drawn in the style of Max Fleischer, with delicate colorings of red, gold and blue. Criselda could hear the last word uttered by our savior, synchronized with the beat of the ceiling fan. It was barely audible, the shadows increasing with each tick of the clock. Criselda had her left hand on the subject's sex organ now, her right hand flicked open the switchblade again. Outside the window, under streetlamps, lovers French-kissed before passing out bored. Lazy hookers fingered themselves and light-bulbs exploded. An illness was preset.

Her playthings were degradation and vice. Criselda had become the vampire of the Atomic Age. Criselda plunged the blade deep into her, just below the sternum. A quick puncture, a surprised look, the prey collapsed into Criselda's arms. Christ continued to mouth unknown words.

"I'm scared now, there is something waiting to touch me, to warn me about my mistakes. At 4 a.m. the panel of accusers will convene to read through the list."

Criselda listened to Cenci's confession. In this manner she neutralized the problem. Sound-snaps were already in progress.

"… and then while he was sodomizing me, I retrieved the autopsy knife I had hidden beneath the mattress. I reached

70

behind me and sliced off his cock on the upstroke on his pullout. He was stunned, maybe confused. Not sure how I should have read his expression. His mouth remained open in a voiceless scream that never ended.

"Not sure how long, everything was slo-mo, he keeled over. While he writhed, I pushed the blade underneath his chin and slowly pushed (a little sound of jawbone scraping and flesh separating, not much, though) and watched it come out his mouth. Fuck, I was sweating. Wondered if there was my juice mixed in with the blood dripping out of his mouth..."

"Always the sound of butterflies. Soft flutter on my clitoris. Am I absolved?"

Sometimes the women were overcome with the urge to remove themselves from the existing scenarios. They would check the current locations of the existing wounds that had ensnared them, trying to determine if a pattern existed. Forensic criminal roleplaying intrigued them. They were in love with the constellations of pain.

The ceremony of her pet's submission affected Criselda in unique ways. Criselda noticed her own handwriting started to change in a myriad of variations: the slant of the letters, the dotting of the *i*'s. It was a vicious pleasure. These things added up until the obsession was overpowering.

The bell rang three times. How does someone know someone? The relationship with her perverts thrilled her. When she made them die slowly for their transactions, she felt whole. Taking their lives with her hands, as she saw the recognition of the death sentence in their eyes, their regrets at knowing that they had destroyed other lives, as well as their own, made her coherent. She knew they shared a sin but Criselda knew her sins were composed of the purity of revenge. It was the essence of cleansing and it made her content.

Whimpering was heard among the clandestine clouds that

were hiding behind the crumbling buildings. Police scanners were reporting random acts of violence. Murders were being committed by solitary perpetrators. It was logical; if there was no partner, there would be no betrayal. The benefits of the drug traveled up the spinal column, making her forget what she did last night. Bloodstained plastic sheets and shiny knives danced in front of her.

One bird was flying solo, crashing into another leather window. Songs minus musical notation. Absent pianos provided a background atmosphere, just a sweet death. Another by-product of a diseased mind tortured by the current fascist government. The Media unspooled images that slapped her in the face.

"You were there too," Criselda said. Her vacant companion gave her the once-over.

"You just didn't care," her friend replied. Touch me there." She motioned towards Criselda's mouth.

"I can see them now," Criselda responded. "Just like you told me a couple of days ago. A guest in a convent that murdered all the guests. Must have been nice."

The two of them stayed locked in Criselda's apartment for 7 days, resting. Foreign eyes glanced at their nude bodies. There was no touching, because Criselda had requested it. The velvet drapes burned. All that they had heard was true.

Forgotten Scenes

In Spring:

The warehouse had been abandoned decades ago when the economy started to fail. It got occasional use from roaming teenage gangs who wanted to cause trouble. Sometimes the noise from their antics of drug use, rape, and murder filled the heavy summer night. Other times it was used as a trysting site for sex maniacs of all genders. Back in 1985 someone constructed an altar out of used televisions and discarded computers. The top was made of broken pieces from the boardwalk that had been destroyed by the last electric storm. It was charming in its own way.

Everything had been prepared, two naked women were draped on the altar. Some boardwalk splinters made their backs uncomfortable. Two spiritual entrées. Muffled screams and faint rustling could be heard behind the scarlet velvet. There was enough seating for a complete orchestra, but only a cellist remained since the other musicians had been slaughtered, the aroma of fresh blood and urine still lingered, mixed in with myrrh. Wisps of smoke caressed the nude women as their eyes rolled back and they breathed deeply. One could still hear voices of anguish, some from the past, some from the present.

The cellist, a Charlotte Moorman of depravity, was clothed in a red satin wasp, her perky nipples were upright. A barbed wire halo was the only other adornment. The only priest present was dangling upside down above the altar, blood dripped onto the nature morte vivante. The women squirmed, but they remained even though they were not restrained in any way. They enjoyed the attention from the sparse audience.

Criselda lifted her skirt, pulled out the switchblade she had strapped to her upper thigh and pushed its button. The blade opened with a satisfying click. The cellist looked a little surprised as the blade entered her throat. Criselda twisted the blade with relish, the musician shuddered and dropped her bow, the cello remaining seated firmly between her legs. Warm vapor and blood gushed out, staining the instrument and floor. After a few moments Criselda removed the knife from the cellist's throat. Criselda lifted Cenci's skirt, pulled down her panties and wiped the blade on her friend's pubic hair. She then put the knife back in its place. Cenci was too surprised to utter a syllable, she just stared at the altar.

The clear light turned Criselda inside out. The bricks were now falling from the cathedral. She tried to steady the tremors in her hands. No success. She sat down and searched for any remaining narcotics in her purse. Finding an ampoule, she cracked it open with her teeth and drank the contents, sucking out every drop. Her cheeks became bellows, drawing on the vial until it was empty. The night-flash started climbing, originating from her spine making its way up into the pelvis, traversing the spine. Flash. Bang. Flash.

She leaned back into blissville and surveyed her mess. The satisfaction of revenge calmed her now. During the preceding events, Cenci wept quietly, finally laying down on the floor, assuming the fetal position.

There is no question that the figure twisted itself off the crucifix and embedded itself inside her. Palms and feet were shredded as the nails ripped through. The faithful were convinced that a miracle had occurred, she wasn't so sure. The agnostics suspected fraud. The obsessed attempted a duplication of the event. Screams could be heard through the renaissance church.

She writhed in agony as the first nail was hammered in. As the process continued, her body twisted and wriggled, and she started to enjoy the pain. Her nerves burned. She adored the feel of the oaken cross against her back.

"Please feed me," she moaned. "Please touch me."

The spectators were so lifelike. She spoke about pain orgies.

"Caress yourself. Put your hands between your legs, run your fingers through my sopping wet mop. Taste your fingers, enjoy the aroma and stickiness. Lacerate your bodies with thorns. We're in the sickness we call Springtime. Cruel thoughts are the new objectives. Love takes roost in the neurasthenic apparatus. Stay with your back against the wall. Don't move just say a prayer or two until the shaking stops."

Criselda's breasts heaved coated with sweat, Blood dripped from hands that were at her side, pooling on the floor. She could see her reflection in the liquid. There were dead on the red canvas. Cenci dropped to her knees leant forward and lapped at the crimson pool, pausing briefly to gag, then started to lick Criselda's fingers (both hands). She relished every drop ad when she was done, she sported a red beard.

"It's going to…"

She sucked each digit clean.

"The periodic table: we're both in there," Cenci said hoarsely. Criselda was charmed by the husky voice, guttural and raw. "We're both in it. My eyes are revolving. We can't leave."

Cenci leaned back so she sat on the back of her legs, thighs clenched. She gazed at Criselda.

"Make me you…" Cenci whispered.

Wicked smiles followed, then just a wicked smile remained.

"Write me something I'll remember. I want kisses of poison." Outside police sirens blared and lights flashed. Criselda had tears in her eyes. Droplets trickled down her cheeks and created rivulets in the pool of gore. A rubbery sound echoed in Criselda's ears, blood rush crashing.

"Society will end with us — you, me and the switchblade as we enter the winter of leather."

Missing love, the bloodied figures clenched each other. Kissing the apparatus of the fallen. Sinister asylums, eradicating the moronic temples.

Visceral minutes past midnight, a slow synthesizer throb was underscoring a tableau of frighteners. Seamed stocking tautly stretched on random female legs, disjointed in the background. In the cafes, the victims are disposed of and hidden underneath the collapsing movie houses. Under art deco crucifixions and scarred clouds, she slept in asthmatic fits tossing/ turning/ tossing her eyes were pierced. Watch out.

Limp pools of water dripped from Planet Venus. She remembered burning nightgowns at the far end of the plateau, where the others had erected a monument to greed. The scenery was singed in preparation for the erotic rites of broken dolls. She hung a necklace of midnight from her neck, finally seeing the real purpose of the blind lunar moths. She kept the creatures just for them. Just for their love.

"Make me you..." Cenci whispered. The creed of the fallen was being created slowly.

Cenci wheezed. The anticipation and the multiple climaxes had kicked in her asthma. She needed to rest for a minute or two. Shaky and lightheaded, she steadied herself against the cracked and stained Pompeii red wall and paused. There was juice dripping down her legs and moisture seeping through a crack in the ceiling, directly overhead. She transformed their logic into other words that neither could understand. Criselda transformed their thoughts into other words, stolen forever. Eyes stared into the rotating moon. Cenci masturbated to 7 more climaxes, as Criselda took photographs. At the end, Cenci collapsed and Criselda sat down. She occupied the time waiting for Cenci to regain consciousness by staring at that stain in the ceiling. It spread. It was dark and intermittently emitted low-fi music.

Their leather lovers nailed their own feet to the floor to please her; she told them to run and laughed hysterically as they screamed in pain, ripping the nails through their feet. As they fell into their own blood pools and wailed in agony, Criselda stared at Cenci, admiring the outline of her lips and the arrangement of her ebony hair around her face. They would never leave. The sweet and luscious radios exploded. She removed the transistors and embedded each one under Cenci's skin. "I love you my sweet Beatrice," Criselda whispered. "You're such a joy, such a toy. Just a frantic Frankenstein Monster, ready to ravage the village."

Random bodies rolled onto a floor of razor talons, their screams perforating the sky. Criselda put her hand in Cenci's mouth and withdrew a severed human finger — a pinky.

Criselda pocketed it and waited for Cenci to sleep her endorphin exhaustion off.

"It will be okay."

Incoherent murmurings annoyed her ears. Fingers with dead nerves caressed her sex organ. "Incredible in so many ways. A nightmare preserved in wax. Let me go now I'm tired. Its beak was inserted deep inside me. the tentacles traveled deep inside me spreading me wide open. Stretched to one more shattering orgasm, until the stained glass fractured."

In the city, the fear grew. Devil doll was in the garden holding a bouquet of bloodstained irises. She seemed vague.

Illicit Pleasures at the Murder Clinic

The pleasure of love that she cherished became ataraxia that she despised. Spitting out names at random cracked windows, victims of burglaries. A gift for the discarded lovers. In the orphaned bar, she fed coins into the jukebox. She adjusted the barbed wire halo around her head and wiped blood from her eyes.

"Don't know why I want to struggle now. I'll lash back. I'll lash back."

A twisted robotic dove slept in her arms last night, providing comfort for her prospective victims. A murderess thinking only of herself, she considered herself affable. There were so many on her list, so many that deserved it.

She awoke early and tried to shake off the previous week's events. She responded to a random mirror in the next room, because that is where her thoughts were hidden from her. Rising from the mattress on the floor, she stretched her arms upwards and outwards, some joints cracked. She reached down and spread her labia apart, trying to perform an inspection. It had been used a lot recently and she felt slightly sore.

"I have to remember to trim my pubic hair, scratchy. scratchy."

Walking to the next room, she stood in front of her favorite full-length mirror and surveyed her body. She was 38-29-38; voluptuous not perfect. Men always wanted her, she knew it. Perfect bait for a perfect crime. She had been fighting depression for years, the "saintly blues," she called it.

"In order for you to change your long-term image, you need to change your life."

She lifted her breasts and let them drop, still firm, they fell into place. Her medium-length black hair was slightly damaged — wrong shampoo or too many dark thoughts. She liked her hair color — it complimented her olive Southern Italian skin tone; her genes came from Calabria and Sicily, with a bit of Piemonte.

She had to assert herself, she had to get moving, she had to tell the fertile dead birds she had many tasks at hand. It was time to get dressed.

Caterina woke from her haze at the faint sound of the intercom buzzer. She had been staring out the window of her third-floor apartment into the end of the late August evening. It had been an overcast day, mid-eighties temperature, very humid. She felt dirty even though she had showered about an hour ago. Her skin was sticky as if she was covered with a very thin layer of invisible scum. She was thinking of showering again before he arrived, but it was no longer possible.

Paura. She remembered that term. A term from childhood; her *nonna* said it often when they watched scary movies on television in their tiny apartment in Rome. She missed her. Now she was thirty-five, still in Rome and earning a very good living as an escort. She liked most of her clients, some were creepy, but most were harmless. Generous old men, who really wanted talking more than fucking. She finished her cigarette and tamped it out in the cracked crockery ashtray, which coincidentally once belonged to *nonna*.

The intercom buzzed again. She walked over to the speaker. Caterina was wearing a see thru peignoir, which provided a glimpse of her black satin wasp, tightly cinched and full-fashioned seamed stockings. Not a totally comfortable outfit, but she felt very aroused wearing it. She hardly ever admitted it, but she did enjoy her profession sometimes. Her high heels click-clacked faintly on the marble floor. This client was one she saw once a week, very nice mature gentleman; always brought her blue irises.

79

"Who's there?" she asked.

"You're favorite. The one who loves you."

Caterina smiled to herself and buzzed him in. She went over to the door and turned the lock, so he could get in; she walked over to the chair in the middle of the living room, and sat down, back to the door. He had a cute fetish. He liked to sneak in and surprise her from behind. She thought that maybe he really did love her. She lit another cigarette and waited. As she blew smoke towards the ceiling, she heard a slight click. Then nothing. Caterina strained to hear more. Nothing.

"You're moving very quietly today, my lover. I'm impressed."

She felt a hand grab her hair roughly and pull her neck back. A hand gloved in black leather covered her mouth. She could smell the odor of old leather, tainted with moisture. Starting to shake, she urinated in her seat. Her arms flailed as she tried to get out of the chair. Another hand grabbed her shoulder and pushed her back into the puddle of pee on the seat, making her feel humiliated. She wasn't used to submission or rough play and her fear turned into liquid blue terror. Her eyes watered, and she wanted someone to help her. No one would be coming, she realized, and she couldn't lift herself up, the strength was too strong.

Caterina started to sob, her repeated stifled screams of "please stop" were muffled by the hand. She managed to bite into it, but the teeth couldn't penetrate the tough leather. The hand lifted off and she managed to get out a scream, but a ball of cloth was shoved deep into her mouth. She started to gag and could feel her eyes bulging as another cloth was wrapped around her head and mouth securing the gag in place. Next, she could feel her wrists being handcuffed behind her. She was in pain. Now she could see the attacker as they turned the chair around. She looked at the face. It was covered by a black mesh, she could barely make out the features. The person was medium height and wearing a black leather trench coat.

Caterina's vagina dripped from terror as she stared at this human who was motivated by depravity. The room was filled by the labored breathing of herself and her attacker.

Caterina made muffled whimpering sounds as the figure stood in front of her. She could feel a cold stare even though she couldn't see the eyes.

"Hello, my pretty-pretty," the attacker whispered. It was a very low whisper.

Caterina started to tremble.

"I have some plans for you my pretty-pretty."

The glint of steel in its left hand caused Caterina to shake violently, attempting to break her bondage. Her head jerked to the left as she was slapped hard in the face. She could taste blood in her mouth. Caterina was now crying uncontrollably, her head bowed. She murmured prayers and thought of her parents in the South.

She felt a burn from the steel as it went from ear to ear. She couldn't breathe anymore, and she heard the hiss of blood as it spurted from her neck and cascaded onto the floor.

It was now midnight.

"So pretty. Such a pretty doll."

The dialogue was directed to Caterina as last remnants of her life drained away. She was barely conscious, and the cuts were excruciating. She was nude. She was suspended by her wrists from the crystal chandelier — a pricey gift from one of her wealthier clients. The heavy leather BDSM restraints from her toybox kept her securely suspended — they were too tight, and her hands were swollen. Her soul was burned out and her eyes were rolled back — instead of her exquisite green eyes only the bloodshot whites were displayed.

The murderer was admiring their handiwork. Neutral thoughts fed through their brain. Caterina couldn't cry anymore; she was so tired and so cold. There was a pool of her blood and urine directly underneath her, a prodigious amount, that reflected the soles of her feet and the twitching of her legs. She struggled to look towards the killer because the glint of steel had brought her back from her almost comatose state. Caterina had the strength to let out one more scream, ripped from the bowels of hell. The murderer had the time to punctuate her wail with a nervous cackle.

The glint of steel came from the autopsy knife that the murderer removed from their pocket. It was held in a shaking black-gloved right hand.

"So much fun..."

Caterina's belly was at eye level and the beast took the blade and slowly inserted it into her tummy on the right side. Deep, a couple of inches, and once that depth was reached started, again slowly, dragging the blade across, slicing skin and muscle. Her remining blood dripped out. Once the incision was completed, her entrails cascaded and landed in a steaming mass on the floor — right into her blood puddle. The intestines were left attached to her corpse. All life had gone.

"It is finished..."

The knife was placed in the pocket and the killer left, whistling in a low tone. the door was closed quietly. The walls of the old building were thick, so no one had heard anything.

A Negative Zero Balance

Criselda woke up with a start. The movie had happened again. It was the nighttime adventure which unnerved her slightly, the one that she had been having since she turned 10. She was walking in a field and feeling irritated because of the pollen. It was sunny, way too sunny — it hurt her eyes and brain. There was throbbing and misadventure in the air. Her crotch felt raw and her fingertips tingled. Then — a slow sensuous rumbling, starting out erotic but quickly becoming frightening. She started walking quickly and the field went from flat to rolling. Rolling hillsides with dangerous teeth ripped at the hem of her short red dress. Her legs were wobbly, but she was able to stay upright. Criselda looked up at spears that were falling from the blank clouds. Moaning. A distant scream. Suddenly the background went blank and two figures stood out in bas-relief. They were moving and passionate. One was a naked mature woman buxom and sweaty long red air flowing in the breeze. She was tongue kissing a creature with an equally voluptuous female body, but this figure had the head of a feminine dinosaur as if designed by Max Fleischer — reptilian in nature but with sensuous lips and long feathery eyelashes. She wore eyeliner and her pale green skin appeared flushed. They stopped their romantic encounter, as their lips parted Criselda could see that a thick mucus web was attached to their lips. They turned to stare at Criselda. Criselda felt their eyes and she felt her crotch tingle as the figures hissed.

As she lay in her bed on the clammy sheets, Criselda pondered the events of the past few days — the hooker murder, the crucifixion, the arrival of Beatrice Cenci — all incidents with sexual overtones maybe there was more, but she could only analyze what the newspapers and television were willing to tell her. She had some friends who were detectives, she would look them up and pick their brains.

The murders were gruesome and fueled by a sexual rage, Criselda reasoned, so the police will suspect a man, but she would study all the angles. Cenci was another matter. Why was she here? Why had she shown up in Criselda's apartment that night? Criselda found her lithe body tantalizing, she made Criselda get back feelings that were thought long dead. But something was off. The phrase she let slip while they fucked "I killed the last one," Criselda wasn't sure it was formed out of twisted passion or Cenci had killed the last lover that gave her an orgasm. Yet Beatrice did not seem capable of these executions. These deaths were planned out and somewhat intricate, fueled by lust, rage and maybe revenge. Cenci did not seem to possess the focus and obsession to create these death tableaus.

"I'll have to study my slight addiction a little more closely," Criselda mused. "She has a way of getting under one's skin — you don't notice it at first and each time feels so good, then the tentacles start unraveling, wrapping themselves slowly around you. The warm body comes closer and the smell of arousal encircles you, then there's the monkey with its fangs in your back."

The Toy hospital. Criselda first noticed the lace one evening when taking a solitary stroll in the warm September air. The shop was closed, but she was able to peer inside the grimy window. The window display instead of being a thoughtful arrangement of elegant antique toys was instead a haphazard array of old discarded playthings placed randomly on different shelves: steel toys, eyeless stuffed dolls, an old cast iron sea captain with the paint flaking off, an African doll with a menacing grin and teeth. Criselda was reminded of "The Steadfast Tin Soldier," and she fought back a teary gasp. She also felt twinge of horror originate at the base of her spine. She liked the tingle of fear it was almost as satisfying as that feeling one gets when sex is about to start. She saw that the shop was open and ventured inside. The interior was just as crowded as the window display, perhaps more so. She half expected a friendly old man or woman to come from the back of the establishment as the bell hanging on the door signaled her entrance. There was no one. Eventually she heard a faint rustle in the back and a yawn as if someone had been napping and was now being awakened.

What followed was unexpected. Criselda heard the click clack of high heels on linoleum and a shadowy figure stepped out of the back and into the dim light. Before her stood a woman in her forties — quite voluptuous, long dark red hair, killer curves encased in a black corset detailed with red brocade. She was poured into a pair of tight leather pants. Her nails were rather long adorned with black shellac. Her skin was white, almost albino, and her eyes were a vacant blue. She stared at Criselda. It was more than a stare — she looked Criselda over from head to toe in a lustful manner that made Criselda a little uncomfortable. The eyes burned through Criselda, almost x-raying her. Criselda pushed her hand into her left jacket pocket and was reassured by the cold switchblade she always carried.

"My name is Aurora. Can I help you?"

"I was just taking a walk and your shop caught my eye. Can I browse?"

"Of course. Just be careful, some of these pieces are very old and quite fragile."

"Thanks, Aurora. I'll be careful."

Criselda walked gingerly through the store, feeing that gaze following her everywhere, watching her every movement.

Criselda felt a flash of light in the corner of her eyes — it came from the glint of a tiny troll doll's eyes. The doll had the familiar off-kilter smile, the hair standing straight up in a red shock. It was nude and happy and in its tiny right hand was a sword tainted with what looked like a blood speck. Criselda smiled to herself, picking the doll up for closer inspection, turned it upside down to check if the horseshoe brand was on one of its soles. And sure enough the mark was there — one of the originals. Since Aurora was not watching her, she pocketed the doll. Shoplifting was something she hadn't done since grade school, when she had been severely punished by the nuns at St. Simon's for the infraction.

She felt someone near her, she caught the scent.

"Anything interest you?" Aurora asked.

No... no... just browsing. I hadn't anything in mind when I came in. I was just lured by your shop window."

"Of course." Aurora went to the back of the store.

"Just shout if you need anything." Aurora slinked off to the back.

Criselda breathed deeply, inhaling the musty odor of the toys. She suddenly started to feel a little frightened. Maybe it was the creepy dead toys or maybe something else. The mix of fear on impending evil started to get Criselda aroused, something which often happened when she was in perilous situations. She had learned to rely on this feeling for safety, so, as she had done many times before, she decided to bail out.

"You know, I have an appointment to get to. I love your store, what are your hours?"

"Oh, we're open every day except Sunday. Noon until midnight."

"Thanks."

"I can imagine what customers she gets around midnight," Criselda thought to herself.

Criselda was on the street now, the faint sound of the shop's door closing behind her. She felt better.

A Scream from a Doll

Beatrice Cenci was sitting on the sofa, smoking a cigarette, when Criselda returned home. Her face was paler than usual, as if she had lost some blood. After each puff she tapped the cigarette several times in the ashtray, as if she was attempting to shake loose an unseen clump of ashes. Each inhalation was deep and she blew the smoke out forcefully. Criselda watched these actions for a minute or two, then cleared her throat.

Cenci was startled.

"Oh! I didn't hear you come in!"

"What are you still doing here? I mean you're welcome to stay, especially if you want to fuck some more, but I thought you had someplace to go. I don't even know where you live."

"I didn't tell you." No other information was forthcoming.

"Okaaay…" Criselda shook her head slightly in amazement. "Difficult girl," she thought.

Criselda noticed that the pupils of her friend's eyes were pinned. That was the reason for her ashen skin and slight tremors of her hands. The voice had that junky drawl also.

"So, you're a user?" she inquired.

"Yeah. So?

"Nothing, just curious. I didn't see any tracks anywhere on your body. Wondering how you ingest that shit."

'I smoke it. My cigarettes are dipped in a heroin solution. Nice and secret. But lately it's not enough. I'll probably have to start shooting it."

"I see…"

Beatrice continued smoking her cigarette, right down to the butt. When finished she carefully placed it into the ashtray.

Criselda went over and stood in front of her. Beatrice's eyes were at crotch level.

"You know I found an interesting store today." Criselda proceeded to tell her friend about the toy store, broken dolls, creepy troll and all.

"I know that place. Used to hang out there when I was a kid. Very creepy. I was friends with one the owner's children. She was a few years older than me. What was her name? I can't remember."

"Aurora?" Criselda offered.

"YES! Yes! How did you know?"

"I met her. Very attractive woman. Luscious and mysterious. A little creepy."

"Yes, she was always a little strange. She liked to torture small animals."

"Torture?"

"Yeah, you know, stick pins in moths and small lizards, burn ants with a magnifying glass, shit like that. I was friends with her for a few years. She went to a different school than me. I always had a crush on her, even before I knew what my feelings were."

"So why did you stop being friends? Because of her sadistic habits?"

"Partly. Time went on and so did the progression of her sadism. She started to scare me. I started stopping by the shop less and less. Then one day I went to the shop and it was boarded up. I heard the family had moved away. I never met her parents, which is strange. Childhood friends usually know the parents. Never found out what happened, but it was rumored that something pretty bad happened and the family moved away. I eventually forgot about her. I always loved that store. We used to play for hours with the toys."

"Well she's back, maybe you should look her up."

"Yeah... Maybe..." Beatrice didn't sound too convincing.

Criselda put her hands in her jacket pockets. She felt something familiar.

She removed the troll she had stolen and held it in front of Beatrice's face.

"Looky... Little Johnny Jewel... he's so cool..." Criselda sang one of her favorite tunes while moving the troll in front of her friend's face. The reaction was unexpected.

"Where the fuck did you get that thing?! Throw it out! Get it away from me!"

Beatrice started hitting the troll, trying to slap it out of Criselda's hand.

"What? Why? What's wrong?" Criselda was taken aback, but she put the troll back in her pocket.

"I stole it from the store. Thought you might like it. Why does it scare you?"

"That thing. That thing!" Beatrice was sobbing now. "Put it away. Please... Please..."

"I always loved trolls. Had a whole collection when I was a kid. I'm sorry. I didn't know they scared you."

She sat down next to Beatrice and hugged her closely. "I'm sorry my baby. My poor baby."

She could feel her friend shaking. She looked at her mascara-streaked face.

"Oh God. Oh God!"

Eventually Beatrice calmed down.

"I'm not afraid of all trolls. Just this troll. I remember it. It was there when it happened. I can't tell you now. I want to sleep."

Beatrice Cenci pushed Criselda away gently then curled up into a fetal position on the couch.

"Please give me music and transparent clouds. I want..." She placed her hands between her legs as she always did when scared. The sexual stimulation made the fear go away. Maybe she would smoke another heroin-laced cigarette or maybe now was the time to start shooting up.

Criselda whispered, "You'll tell me sooner or later."

"No. No. I want..."

"Shhh."

Criselda left her addict lover on the couch, turned off the light and went into the bedroom. She would check on her later. She closed the door behind her, but left it open slightly, in case Beatrice needed her. The preceding incident shook Criselda somewhat since she was not used to being involved in real love affairs. Most of her previous relationships were strictly for sex and fun only, but she was starting to get attached to Cenci.

This was a feeling that she wasn't used to — the twinge of longing for another person.

Criselda turned on her small television and fell back on her bed, sighing deeply. After a few moments, she got up and retrieved a couple of pillows from the floor. She lay back again and propped herself up with the pillows. She used the remote from the nightstand to tun the volume low — in case Beatrice needed her. She clicked through several channels and stopped when she reached the news.

The lead story was the latest murder from the serial killer that was stalking the city since last summer. This latest crime was notably gruesome. The latest victim was a retired school-teacher, a man. Criselda didn't catch the name since the volume was so low. The victim had been cut into pieces. Interviews of former students describing how beloved the mans was followed the murder description. Criselda knew from experience that the cops always held back an important fact about a murder, an old trick to weed out the psychos who always show up after a well-publicized crime to confess.

'Blah blah, fuck!" Just as she was about to change stations, Criselda noticed that the murder had occurred near the toy shop — approximately 2 blocks away. Her spine felt an electric twinge.

The story intrigued her. She would have to do some research on this murder and the previous ones. Criselda changed the channel. After watching a detective movie from the 1940s, she switched off the television. She got up to check on Beatrice. Tiptoeing quietly, she made her way over to the couch. Beatrice was out cold — breathing quietly, still pale white. Criselda left as quietly as she arrived, went back to her bedroom and lay down on her bed.

One story in, one story out — black dances or parades. So sweet, so perverse, so deadly. The people were watching. They knew she was a cheat. They knew what she did. "A perfect bite," she had been told. Teeth in skin teasing the head, then raking over it. Uncontrollable moaning as the tongues progressed. The multi-tentacled thing saw her and it knew. Criselda was clad in a sheer black negligee, everything was on display, but somewhat obscured. The mystery caused her to wet herself. She knew her breasts and pubic mound could be seen. The nipples erect, she was aware of their need for pleasure. Criselda was cloaked in perspiration — the fabric clung to her flesh, outlining her form and her purpose. She knew they were dead, they couldn't hurt her anymore. The humming wouldn't stop. Rapid-fire words folded in upon each other, so nothing was discernible. The figures were intertwined. Her lips were wet. She was embarrassed by the fluid coming out of herself. She had sinned again, she had sinned. The naked man on the crucifix twisted himself to see her in the acts of defilement. It hurts, she knew, it hurt.

Criselda's eyes opened with a start. It had been a rough night of sleeping. Although she hadn't awakened during the night, her body felt as if a truck had run over her. Sore and sweaty, she lay on her back and stared at the ceiling. She studied the cracks in the ceiling. One crack fed into another a swerving pattern that seemed to be in pain, changing direction the longer she stared. One on top of the other. Perversion stories started to emerge in her mind, as they usually did first thing in the morning. They would abate after a few minutes. An infernal march through her brain. Hopefully they would abate. She sighed as she got aroused, but her hands remained clasped on her chest and she closed her eyes. The panic and the lust subsided. Once upon a time.

Gradually she became aware of a distant noise. Humming or buzzing. It was coming from outside her bedroom. With effort, Criselda heaved herself off the bed. She was still wearing her black nightgown — the see-through one that she knew Beatrice would love. Even though she wanted Cenci to leave, she was hoping to seduce her one more time. That woman was such a frantic evil lover — rough yet gentle. Criselda could feel a presence. Out of the corner of her eye she noticed the troll on her bureau. She walked over to it and placed it in the top drawer. The thing made her nervous now.

Criselda opened the door and stepped out into the living room. It was a cloudy day; things weren't very perceptible. She was able to make out a figure kneeling on the floor, staring at the ceiling. Beatrice was saying the rosary. The fingers were clutching the wooden beads with a desperation. Her lips were rapidly moving, words rapidly cascading into each other. Since she was a product of 12 years of Catholic school, Criselda was able to decode the lightning fast Hail Mary: "Hail Mary full of grace the lord is with thee, blessed art thou…"

Criselda stared at Beatrice, mesmerized by the fervor and fear of the supplication to God. After two more prayers, Criselda spoke:

"Ave Maria!"

Beatrice was startled.

"Did I wake you up? I know it's early. Sorry. Sorry."

"No, no, I usually wake up at this time."

"I forget. I'm going. Don't forget to finish praying, my little Leather Nun."

Criselda left the room and walked towards her bedroom. On the way she stopped by the bathroom. On the sink was a used blue tip syringe, it was almost empty, just the remnants of blood mixed with a solution.

"So, the Cenci has given up smoking, gone straight to the source. Bang. Bang. I'm sure there's a bent spoon somewhere."

Criselda sighed, then went back into her bedroom, flung herself on the bed and shoved her face into a pillow. She inhaled the stale smell of sweat and laundry detergent and remembered her bedroom as a child. There was a huge crucifix that hung above her bed which she would stare up at as she would masturbate, edging herself to orgasm. Her earliest memories of sexual arousal were when she would look at the color plates of the stations of the cross. Studying the images of Jesus covered in blood in the musty local church during Easter time never failed to arouse her. The dust was suspended in the air, pierced by sunlight in the afternoons. Always there, it's always there. And there is always murder not far behind. Watch yourself it will happen again. Criselda knew there would be more blood spilled in the next few days. She also felt certain that she had a connection to it somehow. She lifted her face off the pillow and looked at the troll on her bureau. It was still there, grinning at her.

Prayers for Rabid Women

When she finally finished praying, Beatrice remained kneeling, but she stopped staring at the ceiling and switched her gaze to the floor. She looked down at her lithe body, slightly wet with perspiration from the fervor of her religious actions. She thought she would feel better. Even the heroin, which she had injected before her holy ministrations, didn't help. There was that very familiar narcotic warmth, but the flash never happened. Maybe tolerance was building? She didn't know why since she hadn't been shooting very long. Beatrice had smoked the shit for a few months, but shooting it was a new activity — only started a couple of weeks ago.

There was too much happening: her new lover, Criselda, that fear that resurrected itself in a violent fashion when Criselda told her about the toy store and of course Aurora. She wondered how that bitch looked now. She was always very beautiful — even when they were children Beatrice reminisced about their adolescent antics — and that evening that ended childhood forever.

Beatrice stood up for a moment and tried to steady herself by clutching the arm of the couch. Fingernails dug into the black and red patterned cloth. The room became askew and the blood left her face, followed by a cold sweat. She sat down on the couch quickly.

"Too fucking dizzy — too much religion — a nightmare of ecstasy. 'The Little Leather Nun' — I like that name. Very cool. Little Johnny Jewel — Just trying to television. I know that song she was humming. It's pain and loss through and through. I need this."

The Cenci thought about her latest paramour, savoring the images of her body, her vagina and her breasts. That fragrant ebony field between her legs — she loved to nuzzle it and tease the hairs with her teeth. She was so glad she didn't shave like all her other past fucks. The primal image was so much more satisfying. She adored Criselda's odor — a mixture of incense and tobacco smoke — a hermetic combination — a potion for desire. Beatrice envisioned herself in a leather veil and habit (black and white of course). She would look gorgeous and drive everyone crazy as she manipulated the sexual stimulation that co-existed with their religious guilt.

"Oooh — religion — so wonderful, so sensual. Guilt and denial and flagellation. Beautiful tortures of the innocent and the guilty as they writhed. I need to stop thinking like this. I'll climax."

Beatrice turned to the left to look out the window. The apartment was on the seventh floor, so she had an excellent view of the buildings across the street. She admired the mansard roofs and the dirty red brick. The street was bare save for a couple of mundane stick figures slowly proceeding on their predetermined course. The sky was hurting, her pulse quickened for a moment, then relaxed; she stared and stared, hoping to see something of interest. Nothing. Nothing.

There was music coming from an unknown source outside his room. It was a light shrill tune with a light cadence as if a child was singing, but the voice did not really sound childlike. Nicola didn't understand but he was too tired to go and investigate. Too many thoughts floating around in his brain. It had been a very long day of selling his wares on the street. he didn't care who bought them — a junkie was a junkie. He needed money quickly, so he could get out of this mess. He threw his leather jacket on the floor and pulled his shoes off. These were flung into the nearest corner. It had been a nerve-wracking day. Some customers didn't have all the money, so he had to rough them up a bit. One pulled a knife on him, so he had to snuff him out. He wasn't worried, it was nobody who would be missed. Nicola chuckled as he recalled his knife plunging into the guy's belly. Very cool, soft squishy, the look of fear and astonishment on the victim's eyes. It was delicious.

The buzzer rang.

"FUCK!"

Nicola shuffled over to the intercom, stubbing his right big toe on a table leg.

"FUCK! FUCK!"

"Who is it?" he screamed into the intercom.

"It's me, your favorite customer," came the response from a sultry female voice.

Nicola said nothing but buzzed her in. He knew who it was. No, she wasn't his favorite customer, rather she was cloying and a bit annoying. Very sexy, though. Her visits had become more frequent and he was getting a little concerned that her usage might be increasing disproportionately to her finances. He loved the money, but he didn't want to have to deal with another broke addict hanging around. She had offered sex once in lieu of money, but he had refused, not wanting to get into that type of situation; a situation where his sex organ ruled his business decisions. Nicola waited by the door for her arrival. He heard the elevator door open. The doorbell rang.

"Nicola!" A bright cheery smile and ebullient voice always made him suspicious.

"Ciao, baby!"

"How are you doing?" she reached out to hug him and he took a couple of steps back.

"Not feeling too warm and fuzzy, eh Nicola? That's okay. I won't be hurt. I'll make my purchase and leave."

"It's not that, baby. I'm always happy to see you. It's been a long day. Too many fuckin' nutbags to deal with. I feel like my brain has been scooped out and served on a platter."

"Nice image, Nicky."

"Please don't call me Nicky. I love your leather trench coat. Shiny black. Sexy, with a hint of film noir."

She shrugged her shoulders. He walked towards the back of the apartment and she followed sheepishly behind him, her tail between her legs.

They entered the living room and he motioned for her to have a seat. There was a brief uncomfortable silence. Nicola was starting to feel uneasy.

"Glad you like the coat," she said. "I feel so sleek and sexy, makes me wet when I pull it close. Remember when we used to be boyfriend and girlfriend?"

"Yeah, that was fun. Didn't last very long. I was really in love with you, my Demoness. Then you just disappeared. Where did you go?"

She shrugged, asking, "How much for five?"

"Five bags? You got the money?"

"Of course, sweets!"

"Wait here."

He walked into his bedroom on the right and made his way to the big armoire. It was old and musty constructed of oak. A solid piece. He loved it, an inheritance from his *nonna*. After gently opening the doors, he opened the false bottom and took out the merchandise.

Nicola paused in front of the full-length mirror and took inventory of his appearance: black jeans, black turtleneck, red leather vest. He knew he was cool. He was so engrossed in his attire that he only felt the pain when it was too late. Reflected in the mirror, the tip of a stiletto pierced his throat. It had entered from behind, through the neck. Over his shoulder a pair of glaring ebony eyes peered at him, lit up with a maniacal electric spark. It was a slow giggle that evolved into a guttural laugh. She didn't care that his bladder had released, drenching his crotch, legs and her shoes with a torrent of fluid. The aroma of blood and urine hung heavy in the air.

"Smell that? So delicious!" she said.

How had she gotten in here? There was no sound. No sound. What started as a faint crimson trickle quickly meta-morphosed into a red stream of gore spurting erratically. With each beat of his heart the spurts got stronger, splattering the antique mirror, adding beauty to the crazed glass, dripping down, pooling on the floor. As he faded, he hated her.

He saw her face behind his, smiling from ear to ear, as she shoved the blade in deeper and twisted.

"This is so erotic," the Demoness said in a low voice. My cunt is drenched. Fuck, you splattered my coat. I'll take care of that!"

She wiped the blood with her index finger and gave it a taste. When she finally let him fall, she watched in delight as the spirit left his trembling body. His mouth was open — no words were spoken, no sound at all — his face was locked in a blank image of nothingness. The Demoness ignored whatever sympathy she felt for her victim as she painted her lips with the blood from her fingertips. Her black clothing didn't show the blood — something she had planned for. He started to convulse.

"Mmmmmmmmmmmm. Pretty! Pretty!"

The demon hadn't finished her task. As the corpse expired its last breaths, she flipped the body over with a great deal of effort, so that it was lying on its back. The blank eyes amused her, and she paused for a moment to admire her handiwork. Using the stiletto again, she plunged the blade deep, deep into its belly and dragged the blade from left to right. The intestines spilled out, releasing more tantalizing aromas, reminiscent of blood, musk, and semen. She breathed deep and smiled. Feeling capricious, she cut off several feet of gut and hung it from the mirror frame. Like they always say, the penis stays erect. She fondled it until jism spurted.

"Nice! Such a mess!"

She pursed her lips and admired her reflection in the mirror. She bent down and planted a kiss on the corpse's forehead, then closed its eyes. The murderess admired the crimson imprint of her lips. Before she left, she grabbed up the stash of heroin and closed the panel on the secret compartment in the armoire. It had only taken an hour; so much had been accomplished. She wrapped herself tightly in her trench coat and cinched the belt tightly. Slick and snug in a warm womb of black, she was secure.

The combined odors of shit, cum, piss, and blood started to permeate the hallway outside the apartment. When the police arrived the next morning, they were greeted by a trail of red kisses which started by the front door, continued on the walls and ended inside Nicola's bedroom. Each kiss was perfect and evenly spaced. Inside the room the police were treated to a sculpture composed of a corpse, internal body parts and a mirror decorated with body fluids. It was an art installation created by the obsessive-compulsive behavior of a deviant.

A Craving for Sufficient Violence

Criselda had the itch. It was Friday night, 8 p.m. and the yen was back in a filthy fury. The lust monkey was deeply biting into her neck. She left her apartment and took the elevator downstairs, crossed the shabby lobby and re-entered the outside world. No more womb, no buffer. Turning left, she made her way three blocks east and entered the Show Center, home of the Adult Entertainers, Go-Go girls, or as she liked to call them, "The Caged Sexoids." Immediately, she started to feel calmer at the thought of indulging her perverse hobby — voyeurism and anonymous sex. The establishment had a combination of live women in glass booths along with booths that showed a varied selection of pornographic films. There was a menu that the user could cycle through. Each token would allow 5 minutes of viewing.

Criselda loved the film booths, but her favorite were the live peepshows. Each glass booth was in two sections. A customer could enter the glass booth, they were separated from the model by another glass pane, covered by a curtain. Upon inserting a token. the curtain would rise, and the lady would display her wares. An added treat was that by way of a telephone receiver, the customer could chat with the woman. Their lover. Their infernal temptress. The joys of economics.

She adored the women who performed in the glass booths — the peepshows. Criselda's pulse quickened slightly and her pupils dilated as she walked the first floor of the establishment — glass booths one after the other — each cubicle housing a woman — some with eager expressions, a few with a welcoming smile, a couple with a bored "I don't give a fuck" demeanor, many with a vicious cold stare. Criselda's anticipation was rising, but she tried her best to disguise her emotions.

She surveyed the scene. The clientele was composed of mostly males cruising the place, in their mid-forties or older, looking embarrassed, eyes darting around, imagining that they actually had a chance of sexual interaction with any of these women. Their hands fondled some tokens — each one would make the curtain between them and the model rise for one minute. The most they could hope for was a glimpse of a finger in a cunt. No touch, no taste, no smell. She randomly searched her festering mind for a comforting portrait, someone safe. Unlike the others, she considered her trip an intellectual exercise.

"Hello. Criselda, isn't it?"

Criselda, startled, turned around quickly. Her hand reached into her blazer pocket, fingering the stiletto she kept for emergencies. She relaxed a bit when she realized it was Aurora from the antique toy store.

"Oh, hi! Sorry, you scared me. I didn't expect to meet anyone I knew here."

"Me neither."

Criselda glanced at the newspaper Aurora was holding.

"Anything interesting?"

"Yeah, actually. A gruesome murder last night. Really fucking bloody. Nasty. It was someone I sort of knew through business."

Their conversation was punctuated at intervals by moans and obscenities emanating from the peep booths.

"Let's go outside. It's hard to hear sometimes in this place," Criselda said.

Standing in front of Show Center, unashamed and smiling at the random men scurrying quickly into the establishment, Aurora and Criselda continued their conversation.

"Anyway," Aurora continued, "A drug dealer, Nicola, was found murdered in his apartment last night. He was cut to pieces. I had some dealings with him over the years. Just some pot, no hard stuff, but I knew he dealt junk and meth and probably mixed with some very desperate characters."

"What was his last name?"

Aurora looked away into the space behind Criselda

"Uh not sure. Wait! I remember now. Salerno. Nicola Salerno."

"Hadn't he and his girlfriend been accused of throwing a woman off the roof of an apartment building a few years ago? Drug deal gone way wrong. Something like that, right? The cops had done a poor job in the arrest, no reading of rights, chain of evidence broken, so the case was thrown out. Usual fucked up shit. Those guys are so corrupt. I remember hearing that Nicola had friends on the police force. His girlfriend disappeared. She was young in her early twenties and she left without a trace. Always dressed in black. Shoulder length black hair. Supposedly a real stunner. The press dubbed her "The Noir Demoness" — would make a great band name. Nicola supposedly went back to dealing with relative immunity because of his police friends."

Aurora was listening in rapt attention. Criselda felt that she was not only interested in the facts but also in her body.

"Interesting! I do remember hearing about the girl on the news several years ago. The paper said he was brutally murdered, blood and semen splattered everywhere. It looked like the ejaculation occurred after death. I guess he went out smiling — sorry."

Criselda smiled. She saw that they shared a common sense of humor.

"Also, some words were written on the walls, but no other details were given."

Criselda took note that Aurora was getting a little pleasure from the grisly details of the case. She also took note of their mutual attraction.

"I really love your shop. It's quite unique. I've always had a fascination for antique toys."

Both women were standing, but Criselda needed to shift in place a little, she felt herself getting moist and she thought that somehow Aurora knew this, as if she could smell the arousal.

"I'm so happy you're interested in my shop. So many people think it's a waste of time. I barely break even, but I love it. Please come and visit me again. By the way, you can keep that blonde troll you lifted from the shop. It's very dear to me, but I want you to keep it because I think very soon you will also become important to me. My special one."

Aurora came up close and placed her left hand gently between her companion's legs. As her face drew near, Criselda could see images of ecstatic copulating purple satyrs in the woman's pupils. There were clouds overhead in the night sky, throbbing and silent, kissed by the moon. Criselda's eyes widened as Aurora leaned in and whispered into her left ear.

"Very special."

In Negative Space

This day was Wednesday. Criselda awoke with a start — maybe from a nightmare, but she couldn't recall. Her eyes were open, but not recognizing images. She thought of Aurora's eyes and glanced at the clock-radio: 6 a.m. Way too early. She attempted to go back to sleep but couldn't. The apartment was empty, had been for several days. The Cenci hadn't come back and Criselda was starting to feel depressed.

"Shake it off. Shake it off."

Maybe she would go visit the toy store today. She yearned to see Aurora, but she was apprehensive. Criselda also craved Beatrice, but this scared her also since she didn't want to be dependent on anyone or anything. Frustrating. The battle for love and attention. The yearning between her legs. It all hurt. The monkey was biting. The nebula of neurons that surrounded her and her environment was choking her. She wanted desperately to leave forever, hide in a place where no one knew her. That's what had brought her to this place, but she was starting to make acquaintances and wanted to run away again. This city was delivering nightmares into her bloodstream. She counted her breaths, trying to get back to sleep.

"This way. This way."

On cue, she heard the front door open. By instinct she searched for something she could use to protect herself. Her knife was in the jacket thrown across the chair on the other side of the bedroom. She reached under her bed and felt for the baseball bat she had hidden there. Criselda pulled the bat under the covers with her. Sleep baby sleep. Clutching it in her hand she held her breath for a second and listened for further indication of a life form in her home. Nothing. Sound had evaporated. She observed that it wasn't that the sound had disappeared, but everything was empty, as if it was this film that had no soundtrack.

Criselda detected the slight sounds of birds outside her windows. Automobiles were cruising by; the city had started to rise from its grave. Soon the zombies would start stumbling toward the train and bus stations, flagellating themselves as they wandered off to their jobs. Her mood dipped slightly, so she started to finger herself — her antidepressant. When her mood shifted upwards again, she stopped masturbating.

Sound came back in a whoosh reverse of a jet engine — rockets shot between her eyes. Black wings wrapped themselves around her body and hot lips smothered hers. A cold hand was pressed between her legs forcing them apart. She was still wet from her recent attempt at self-pleasuring and was embarrassed somewhat for being caught in this situation. Somehow, she had lost her grip on the baseball bat and it was now in the sheets somewhere. This was a female creature. Criselda smelled her — odors of arousal and the smell of blood on windowpanes. Cracking nails screeching on slate.

A cigarette-damaged voice asked her, "So, where is it, my sweetie?"

"I don't know."

Criselda was not comprehending; her body was soaked from fear and arousal.

"I'm going to put the frighteners on you my so whorey horny baby."

It was difficult for Criselda to discern what was attacking her — just a swirl of black punctuated with crimson and purple. It hurt and gave her a climax simultaneously. Something was being drawn out of her — liquid pain and desire. What was this thing looking for? It was female, she thought. I don't understand. Criselda felt guilty for no apparent reason — the walls absorbed the sound. Her voice was gone.

The subtlety of this creature's voice licked the inside of her brain and messaged her spinal cord. Implied over explicit violence.

"He was conceived by the power of the Holy Spirit and born of the Virgin Mary..."

Criselda tried to stiffen her back and wrestle her arms free. She was pinned to the bed. The claustrophobic lover was burning. She thought of Beatrice. She was most likely roaming the streets looking for another drug or another fuck or both.

> *"He descended to the dead.*
> *On the third day he rose again.*
> *He ascended into heaven..."*

Vacuum. pain. Neon lightbulbs twirled and the movie marquee screamed. Holes in her crotch — in the celluloid — a white-hot ripped circle trapping them both. Gentle hands caressed her face. Thoughts went way way back. Parched lips.

Sound back again. The creature had disappeared, Criselda caught a glimpse of a leather clad thing running out her bedroom door. Criselda jumped up, barely clothed, ran down the hall after it. She saw a black blur make its way out the front door. Criselda stood outside her apartment, nearly naked, looking up and down the hallway. She was alone.

"He will come again to judge the living and the dead..."

Fever mirrors, murmurs from a female unleashed, high-strung and rabid with revenge. She was foaming at the mouth and frothy between her thighs. The crown of thorns was woven with meticulous care and infinite patience. When completed, she smiled. When finished she raised it high so God could see. She kissed it gently and roughly shoved it onto the head of her first victim. One thorn poked through the flesh of the forehead. Her lover, her prey writhed in pornographic splendor. She knew why. Her lover preferred the shadows, that was the sin.

They sat, clad in leather, in front of the television, wide screen, throbbing, watching the ballerina burn. It was a delicate auto-da-fé. The pyre of twisted nerves and soundless agony blazed across the ceiling. The marquee was bare — blank — no words of symbols of communication. The kingdom of light. The last fuse had blown.

Every murder followed her, she was fleeing like a twisted vixen in heat, she couldn't endure one more fuck, one more climax, still she craved it until she was raw. She was casting for the perfect film. She needed three more actors. Dial 911. Criselda was attacked more and more by these memories. She didn't even remember what the reason was, where they came from or what she had been hoping to accomplish. Her heart hurt, not metaphorically. It was a brutal ache. She missed Beatrice dearly. Criselda was afflicted by the true pain of longing for her lover. "This isn't good," she thought. I'm living on quicksand now. Beatrice has me now. It hurt even more since she realized that Beatrice wasn't reciprocating. She came and went at random, as she pleased. Truly selfish.

Analgesic Beasts of Eve: The screen split. Moan.

Criselda entered the room. There was a stool in the center of the room. Five feet in front of the stool was a shiny steel bucket, the kind that professional kitchens use to carry sauces. Against one wall was a black leather couch set up to view the stool and pail. Criselda could smell the leather. A 1935 Philips radio (floor model) was in the right corner behind her. She wore high patent leather heels ca. 1945 and had an iron taste in her mouth. Her body was draped in gauze, her long black hair was slightly damp and above her upper lip was a thin line of perspiration. She drew her shaky fingers through her hair in frustration, slowly pulling out a few strands as part of the process.

"Sing. Song. Show."

Overhead was a circular fluorescent bulb.

"Pale." She raised her hand in front of her eyes. The light traced the capillaries in her finger webs.

She walked towards the stool; /click /clack as her heels touched the waxed parquet floor. She briefly admired the intricate designs under her feet.

She sat down.

She hummed a monotone note as she stood up and stood over the pail. Slowly a strong stream of hot urine flowed into the receptacle. When done, she lifted the pail above her head, continuing the monotone note repetition. After her offering, and with legs spread apart, she poured the contents onto the floor. The squiggly creatures (furry and moist) that were inside her Bakelite retinas became manifest and perched on the couch to watch. She stopped humming and sat down.

"My, my, gentlemen. A dollar from each of you please." No release.

Something was vocalized from the love canal. She reached inside and thought awhile, looking up at the sheet metal ceiling and licked her black fingernails.

"A sharp tingle to overflowing."

She screamed and bent over, begging forgiveness. The figures on the couch were silent.

The jury never had a verdict. The fluorescent flickered occasionally and buzzed slightly. Other females entered, naked and silent, to sit on the couch and watch the show. She had nothing to give them. The iron taste grew stronger as she darted her tongue quickly between maroon lips. The screen split once more and she fell backwards. The furry beings were on top of her, snickering and clicking as they took what they came for: pieces of skin, hair, gauze, so they could construct stick dolls. Figures constructed, she was barren.

Radio on.

The naked women touched each other and dreamed as their eyes rolled backwards, naked backs sweaty / sticky on the couch.

"The music is too loud," the middle woman said. The woman on the left got up, walked toward the radio, switched the radio off, and then tasted her fingers.

The woman on the right smiled.

Criselda lay still.

Angelic Beasts of Eve

The straight razor had done a perfect job of removing the mother's face. The woman, Alessandra, had been home all day, her neighbors stated. It was to be a day off to relax. The children were visiting her mother for several days and her husband was on a business trip and wouldn't be back for a week. She had been looking forward to sleeping late, streaming her favorite shows and eating what she wanted to eat. Her neighbor came over to borrow some money since she wanted to make a quick stop at the fruit stand at the corner and couldn't locate her purse. Not wanting to go all the way to the bank, she decided to hit up her friend for a small loan. The front door was slightly ajar and there were a few red spots on the top step. The neighbor was greeted with a gruesome tableau: a new definition of "altarpiece."

The body had been dismembered with cruel precision and arranged on the oak dining room table. The arms and legs had been separated from the body and the head was decapitated. As stated previously the face had been removed with delicate clean cuts, exposing a twisted visage of underlying facial muscle and gore. All the body parts were reassembled into the shape of a cross with the torso in the center. The head with neck attached was inserted into the torso, the completed assembly resembled a demonic pinwheel that one would see in a S. Clay Wilson Zap comic.

There was an odor of blood and freshly cut meat permeating the house. The coroner estimated that the vile incident could not have occurred more than 3 hours prior to the discovery.

The neighbor, Aurora, who spoke to the police, described herself as a casual acquaintance of the deceased. "We would see each other in the street every so often and exchange pleasantries. We weren't that close, but she was very nice. I could tell she loved her family. I own and manage an antique toy store and she had promised to pay my business a visit, since one her children's birthdays was coming up and she was shopping for a present."

Aurora was very composed when speaking to the press and the *polizia*. Her eyes darted nervously, and she licked her lips more than one would expect, betraying an underlying tension.

She noticed that the walls and the floor of the dining room were splattered with blood almost reminding her of a very crimson Jackson Pollock creation. Surprisingly there were no footprints or handprints. This murder required a lot of movement, maybe the killer had cleaned up the signs of their presence. The traits of an experienced artist of death.

Beatrice thought, "Let's return to domestic bliss: Another Night for an American Wife."

Black streets. Black vision.

Fluctuations.

She smiled to herself as the animals screamed in unison, not recognizing her.

The walls of the houses were ebony. The marquee was gray. The letters were scarlet and blurry. Beatrice couldn't read the film's title.

She had purchased a ticket but didn't understand things, how it all fit together. She clutched the ticket tightly in her hand, soaking the paper with her sweat. Her black fingernails bit into her palm, almost drawing blood. She could hear the blood rushing in her temples as her stomach grew bitter.

She was outside in the seething mist at 8 p.m., a normal time for a show to start. She peered in through the glass doors. In the lobby the poster frames were vacant.

The box office was closed again, and she didn't understand

how she had procured a ticket. Her leather boots were scuffed. Her leather skirt was torn. Her leather mind was spasming, but the door was open, and she walked into the theater, stopping briefly in front of the box office to stare at her reflection in the black glass — the glass that had a vacant stare behind it. A shimmering faint green wisp appeared briefly behind the glass, then faded as slight noise touched her eardrums and an odor of burnt hair tickled her nostrils. They spoke to her. She was wet deep inside and fear was incrementally growing. Hoping that no one noticed she gently caressed her vagina then tasted her fingers.

"I can't stop doing it."

She ignored her senses and walked down the hallway.

"They're looking for me," she whispered to herself. Her mouth tasted of blood, she spit into her hand to see if her saliva was red. She stared at the crimson puddle gathered in her cupped palm. It pulsated slightly. She brought her cupped palm up to her face and inhaled the mixed aroma of blood and vaginal fluid.

"My name is Beatrice," she whispered to herself.

Her wrists had red marks all around them.

"Pretty bracelets. Pretty bracelets. I had to do it."

A fraction of the universe was sliced off by a knife. Severe thin cold fingertips gently, lightly caressed her face as she walked down the hallway to the cinema gently touching the pock-marked plaster walls. She couldn't discern the colors of the walls. She was greeted by dank sounds and mildew wafting past her face.

Beatrice was startled when she came up against a heavy velvet curtain. She breathed deeply and gingerly stepped past the decay and into the theatre. She could barely make out the seated figures that were staring at the screen. Looking straight ahead they paid her no notice. She sat down in the last row. The screen was blank.

"They want to get into my pants, they want to take me away."

She frequently desired to see her face, so for the 7th time that evening she reached into her purse and took out the cracked hand mirror she always carried with her. As she admired her image's reflection, two red orbs appeared, superimposed over her hazel eyes. Beatrice smirked at the image, gently licked the mirror and placed it back in her purse.

"Desire."

As she sat in the theatre, her flesh started to slightly tingle. Gentle pale hands were caressing her thighs, she could feel it as she squirmed in the seat. The hands had appeared spontaneously, having been dormant for so long. Their owners had smelled her and they had arisen. She looked down — a pale wispy female face was smirking at her, white plasma dripping from its lips. It mouthed words that she couldn't understand yet were faintly remembered from another incident. Translucent in the extreme, the face rose up slowly, revealing that it was attached to a willowy translucent body that eventually straddled Beatrice and wrapped her arms around her. The figure's tongue, moist and white, licked her eyelids and gently worked Beatrice's lips apart.

Beatrice had never been as aroused as she was at this particular point in time. A thousand clocks gently ticked and outside on the street the animal chorus was aroused again. When the figure had finished, it vanished, and Beatrice realized that she was sitting in a puddle of mutual female juices and white goo.

"They want to get into my pants, they want to take me away."

A whirr of a projector drew her out of her reveries and she

once again stared at the red marks around her wrists. Her skin was clammy now instead of being flushed. The walls were still breathing, and a knife fell from the ceiling landing in the seat next to her. A gift from the mother of all those present.

"Use it," was whispered into her left ear.

A slender female shadow, clad in latex, wrapped in pleasure, spoke again.

"Use it for me."

The figure's breasts heaved under the synthetic flesh. Her eyes burned through the latex and accused Beatrice, who orgasmed twice. A national climax.

The only thing she desired right now was for the film to start. Whips cracked in the background, in the space behind her head. Her forehead was burning, and her ebony hair was damp. There was exhilaration among the patrons as the projector whirred, illuminating faint particles of dust in the space above her head. Several seated figures slowly clapped faintly. There were no previews, straight to the main feature.

She prayed as her skin glistened in the faint light and the sounds of leather punishing skin subsided; ebbing pain and slow smiles were present in the air. Several butterflies collapsed on the floor around her and she ground their bodies into the wooden floor with her vinyl black stiletto boots. They only screamed for a moment, but disturbed the other patrons, who were discovered to be female, pale and in possession of glass-like eyes that burned through the darkness.

Beatrice took the knife that had fallen earlier, flicked it open and drew slight lines over her red wrist marks, just enough to draw blood. Faint crimson always made her smile.

A narration droned:

"We are born into here screaming and we leave here screaming. Some leave quite vocally, some in a more subdued fashion, but there is always the scream: external or internal — it's all the same."

"Welcome to the plague years."

The stink of the subway, the specters' slime on board, some in shock some too stupid to realize what is going on. A mistake forever.

The scantily clad women from nubile to way past prime are there also. Some breathe heavily, heaving. In heat. Somnambulism.

"Are you ready?" a woman said.

Smiling, she put the gun in her mouth and pulled the trigger. The night was crimson. The dark smelled of plasma and heat.

"He walked home having lost her love. The streets, wet after the rain, crunched ever so softly under his boots."

"Divine revelation from the night," the spectators chanted.

Bombarded by these sensations, Beatrice rubbed between her legs as she usually did when in a panic. Her fingers reached under her skirt, parted her labia, and she fucked herself raw. The pleasure washed over her and she felt slowly drained as her wrists bled. The spectators cheered and floated gently over her head in front of the screen.

Her eyes rolled upwards, she spasmed cold and fearful. Afraid, she panted, and her legs shook. Sweat rolled down her thighs. One tear fell from her left eye.

One of the figures tongued her ear, gently intoning, "Divine revelation from the night. I love you."

She was hers. The clocks ticked louder, and the sounds of whipping had ceased.

Beatrice was now wrapped in black gauze.

"The streets looked funny yesterday."

"Pretty bracelets."

"Can't tell one from the other."

"Pretty bracelets."

"I had to do it."

"I love you all."

The audience filed out, back to the black houses. The projectionist was never seen again.

"As always, I want to go to my room now."

Her name is Serena Fiore, Beatrice Cenci is not her birth name. Her brain had been raped by the literature and images of Antonin Artaud, so she renamed and remade herself in the image of the tortured noblewoman.

"I don't think, I just move seductively in an enchanted magickal manner. I rarely sleep and I love to pleasure myself. Orgasms and blood."

Beatrice laughed to herself. Those were words she used to repeat to herself when she reached puberty, when the rooms were empty when mamma and papa were away, when she entertained herself with horror literature and exploitation movies on TV or the kind she would smuggle in to play on the VCR. Serena would visit the video store every week or so and shoplift what she wanted. The owner being nearly blind, never knew what was going on. Serena hid the cassettes under her blouse or coat, depending on the weather. Once at home, she would lay the booty on her bedspread and admire them. They were totems that offered her into a new world of gods and monsters, also sex and death. She was creating new vistas where her mind could travel, sucking up the images from the exploitation and grindhouse films. She craved the experience to view these movies in an authentic rundown theater that smelled of piss, blood, and cum.

She would sit, in rapt attention, staring at the television screen. Scheming, dreaming and fondling the stiletto switchblade (her favorite toy) — the one with the 6-inch blade. Serena had snatched it off some sleaze bag who tried to fondle her. Instead of an evening of passion, she kicked him in the testicles and poked his eyes with her fingers. Laughing maniacally, she plucked the knife out of his coat pocket and ran away. A very fulfilling and satisfying evening.

Blowup — a catalogue of sins examined in high resolution. Close-up of her eyes as she watched her fingers at work. Demonic black and white or maybe sepia stills of the aktion: a knife plunging once or twice. Tell me why you did it. Talk to me. Please. The sound, any sound comforted her.

Eyeliner and mascara applied — skin tight leather dress. She was morphing. Blades cutting up the sky. A myriad, a piece of pain, stitched together once more. She feels she felt.

Reminiscing about the love and terror cult. Manson and the girls just as LIFE had described them. She felt.

Always hard to sleep — the creatures in the black rooms won't pray for me. Why is silence better? Those cold stares as I walk home — only sounds from random traveling transistors circa 1969. Behind the curtains — the saints cried. La Papesse screamed.

And finally falling on her back, exhausted, sweaty, her fingers damp her cheeks flushed. Next, she felt the blood drain from her head, she could feel the clamminess approaching. always happened this way. Always. What would come next? Beatrice Cenci — the young and gorgeous noblewoman, victim of abuse, enjoyer of parricide. Serena was her and she would get revenge. Under the mantle of her image Serena would forge new methods of murder and mayhem. They would notice her. These were dreams that would be realized later, but for now she would be transitioning into Beatrice Cenci.

At age thirteen she started to become fixated with the antique toy store down the block from the house that her parents loved. They would raise a happy family together as Man and Wife. Husband and Possession. It was at the end of a cobblestone street, very narrow and dark. The store was old, the window was a reliquary of broken doll corpses. Slaughtered pieces of old and new dolls originating way back long before Mattel and Hasbro or Ideal.

"I need the totems from my past I need the wounds that my time forgot."

She remembered wistful images with a slight tinge of fear at the base of the spine, deliciously tingling, working upwards. Beatrice was fascinated always with the murders and the disgrace, the heat and the pain. A gorgeous female in rapt attention watching the new violence of current events that the television fed, black and white glory of culture's descent into madness. Spahn Ranch sonatas, abject crescendos, all defiled and defamed. The girl couldn't help it. She was born to love it. Creepy crawly — make it witchy. The murders ran their own course: unstoppable and uncontrollable. Sealed in heaven with a kiss. The venom that she collected in memories wasn't enough to satiate her.

Lurid melodramas made her wet, the earliest tingling of approaching adulthood. Technicolor writhing on the dirty stained linoleum floors. She relished the risqué. Crescendos of moans from a gibbous moon, sweet penetration of limp fabric. Slowly. Slowly now. As she slowly again uncrossed her legs, lithe warm endeavors of an entrapment until the silence overloaded, overwhelmed — white noise — humming — giggles — slight indications of bells so far away. This door had been closed. Locked now. Eyes bled crimson tears no sound anymore. Corruption had become rampant.

"My lovers, I miss you so much. Fuck!" she said. "I'm done but have to keep going. I hate this pain, yen upon yen, burning skin then cold flush. Puking out forgotten memories."

As the fluid hit the water, music sprung. With each gasp she remembered what she craved to forget.

"What did I do with you after fucking you? There was no more need of you. Threw you away, limp and lifeless."

Beatrice wiped her lips, then splashed her face with icy water to revive. Manic sounds and activities were becoming exhausting. She went back to that antique toy store. What's the name? *Forgotten Memories.* The story always changed. Creeping down the street, having snuck out of her house up the block, those toys drew her in. Beatrice peered through the dirty glass. Toy upon crippled toy piled up.

Just yesterday Beatrice had picked up another one. Handsome young man. They had met in the coffee shop near Criselda's place. Beatrice was drinking espresso slowly; she loved the way her heart pumped when the beverage coursed down her throat. A warm stream down then a bang as her spinal column jolted into action. She saw him sneaking a peek at her. This was the one. He was about twenty, short brown hair. His slight frame made him appear weak and vulnerable. She smiled at him when she finally caught his eye. He had blushed and looked down at his feet. Beatrice motioned for him to come over and sit with her. Hesitantly he ventured over and took a seat across from her.

"Don't sit way over there, come sit next to me."

After he changed his seat, she put her hand on his knee and gave it a quick squeeze. He wasn't expecting that.

She fluttered her eyelashes many times — she remembered an old move from the seventies that she really loved – *Mistress of Depravity*. She had become a Mistress of Seduction.

"My name is Persephone," she said. Beatrice never used her real name with them. Only Criselda knew her real name.

"Alessandro."

She said it was a cute name, although she didn't really like it.

"Would you like another espresso?" he asked.

"Yes please. A double."

He came back with the double for her and the single espresso for him. She stared at him for several seconds before sipping at her beverage. She rolled the black fluid around her mouth and breathed in as a wine connoisseur would do, enjoying the fragrance of the coffee. Finally, she swallowed. The caffeine mixed well with the joy bang of heroin she had done earlier. An opioid locomotive traveling through her nervous system. When would this stop?

"Do you take any recreational drugs?" she asked.

"Only pot."

"Good Boy Scout. Pussy." Alessandro blushed again. "What a schmuck," she thought. "I'm sorry," she said.

"Anyway, if you want to come home with me, you have to watch me shoot junk — or are you too afraid?"

He seemed frightened but eventually stammered that he would go with her. He was desperate.

"Do you live far from here, Persephone?" Cute, he remembered her name.

"No, just around the corner."

Beatrice had rented a cheap room at the run-down art deco hotel around the corner from the coffee shop. It was a gorgeous structure in its prime, built in 1927, but those days were long, long gone. Originally a hangout for the more successful artistic types, it had become a haven for the lost. She missed Criselda's apartment, but she wouldn't bring Alessandro there, Criselda would make him very uneasy. Plus, she didn't want Criselda to know anything about her own needs.

She grabbed his arm as they left the café and they walked arm in arm out the door. She sensed he was becoming more relaxed and comfortable, which nauseated her slightly.

Alessandro seemed a little startled at the site of the dive.

"Don't worry baby, it's a cool place."

Beatrice led him into the front entrance. They walked past the vacant front desk and down towards the back.

"I like where the room is situated," she told him. "No one can hear us, and we won't hear anyone. The clientele gets a little noisy in the evenings."

She had a little difficulty opening the door to her room, but eventually got the key to work. Once inside she kissed him passionately and attempted to touch his closed teeth with her tongue. Eventually he loosened up and their tongues touched. he wasn't a bad kisser, but he needed practice.

"Relax man," she said. "It'll be okay."

The room was a studio with a sad bed and a very small area

which served as a makeshift kitchenette, just a table with a hotplate, a sink and a single cabinet. In the back was a small bathroom with a shower, no bathtub. Near the bed were a couple of chairs and a portable television on a rolling stand.

"Sit down, please." Beatrice motioned for Alessandro to take a seat, which he did without saying a word.

Beatrice produced a black scarf from her jacket pocket.

"Alessandro, I'm going to blindfold you for a few minutes. I don't want you peeking, or you'll have to leave. Do you promise to keep the blindfold on?"

He nodded his head meekly. Beatrice tied the scarf tightly around his head, covering his eyes. When she was done, she let the fingers of her left hand graze his crotch. He was aroused, a fact which made her depressed.

Alessandro could hear her moving around, random noises of shoes and clothes falling to the floor and boxes being moved. After a while she removed the scarf brusquely.

He blinked his eyes several times and was overcome with the image before him. Beatrice was standing in front of him. She was nude except for a pair of black leather thigh high stiletto boots. She was fingering her neatly shaved pussy. He couldn't take his eyes off the rabid black triangle between her legs and the sight of her fingers going in and out the wet hole.

"Do you like my physique?"

Beatrice stretched her arms above her head so he could admire her form.

"Yes, you look very healthy!"

Beatrice started laughing, then stopped suddenly.

"These boots once belonged to a friend of mine. She was an exotic dancer — actually, she was just a stripper and a prostitute. She was a good soul. She's dead now. The cops don't know why or who. She was found with her throat slashed in Manhattan, near the Westside Highway. It was horrible — she was scalped, too. When they tried to move the body, her face fell off. We worked together sometimes — sharing jobs and johns. I know she was into some kinky scenes and I'm sure her extracurricular activities got her snuffed."

As she spoke her fingers moved rapidly. Her deep red fingernails glistened under the fluorescent overhead.

"Can you imagine what that looked like? She always wanted to go to Vegas, to dance professionally."

To Alessandro it seemed as if she was about to climax.

Beatrice calmed down suddenly.

"You said you would watch me shoot up. Then we can fuck."

To her amazement, Alessandro agreed by nodding meekly.

"Okay, baby. I'll get the works."

Beatrice strode off to the kitchenette, his eyes followed her slinky form as her ass wiggled and the stilettos heels click-clacked on the soiled linoleum floor. Her shadows danced on the walls under the sickly light. His eyes followed them. He didn't want to tell her it was his first time. He was ashamed of his innocence but tired of watching internet porn and fantasizing about women who were never there. He would pray for his sins then resume the whole cycle every day. After the pain of 12 years in Catholic schools, nuns and brothers, he had finally decided to shun it all and indulge. He wanted a dangerous female and Persephone was the one. He would do whatever she wanted.

Alessandro's eyes stayed with her, following her every move, every flex of her body. Her skin was glistening. He craved to touch her fingers and savor the sweet smell of her hair. He was certain her hair had the aroma of sweat.

Alessandro's reveries were interrupted by Beatrice.

"Are you okay?"

She touched his right cheek gently and smiled.

"I have the stuff. I'll be ready in a few minutes."

She showed him a small wooden box. It was ebony and very old. She removed the lid and displayed the contents: a few diabetic syringes, some cotton balls, a leather thong, a bent spoon, a cigarette lighter and a few glassine envelopes containing a white powder.

She gingerly took each item of the box as if she were handling holy relics.

"These syringes are brand new. They're the best too. I swiped them from the emergency room last time I was there. I had brought in a friend who had tried to slash her wrists. She made such a commotion that I was able to steal the needles — blue tip lure lock. They go in real easy."

The last item she removed was a glassine envelope that was stamped with the image of a bleeding eyeball.

"I'll be ready soon."

She went to the sink and returned with a glass of water.

Beatrice opened the envelope and emptied the contents into the bent spoon. She took one of the hypodermic needles and filled it halfway with water. After squirting the water into the spoon, she used the cigarette lighter to heat the spoon until the solution boiled slightly. She placed the spoon down on the table and let it rest on the bent handle. A tiny ball of cotton was dropped into the solution. Beatrice took the needle, inserted it into the cotton and slowly sucked up the fluid. She tapped the barrel of the syringe to remove the bubbles and adjusted the solution with the plunger. When everything was ready, she put the syringe down on the table and smiled.

"Alessandro, can you hand me the leather tie from the box?"

Alessandro dutifully brought over the leather thong and handed it to her. She made a loop and tied it around her arm above the elbow.

"My veins are near the surface, makes this really easy."

She pointed to the vein that was bulging.

"This is the 'median cubital vein' — I asked a doctor once. It's the best vein for drawing blood and injections.

Taking the syringe, she inserted the needle into the vein.

"You know, I can feel a slight pop when the needle hits the right spot. Look at the flowers."

The blood blossomed into the fluid slowly, she pulled back on the plunger several times. Finally, she released the thing and became very quiet.

"Oh man..."

Beatrice's eyes rolled back, her legs still clad in the black leather boots were wide open. The needle was dangling from her arm. Alessandro didn't know what to do.

"Persephone? You okay?"

After a few minutes Beatrice came to, pulled out the syringe, and threw it to the floor.

"Come over here and get on your knees, pretty boy."

He had never imagined this scenario as his first time, but Alessandro was excited and rock hard. He crawled over to Beatrice and kissed her lips, which were slightly cold. He licked her neck and dragged his tongue down her torso until he reached navel. He tongued her navel and made his way to her cunt. Her pussy was already wide open, and he attempted cunnilingus as best he could remember from the internet pornography he had watched. She moaned and stirred.

"No stop. I want to suck you. Get on the bed."

He went over to the bed and removed his clothes. Beatrice walked over somewhat unsteadily as she felt the junk rush through her body. She got on the bed and grabbed his erect cock. She smiled — it was big enough — and proceeded to lick the shaft and the balls, working her way up and down, pausing to suck on the head occasionally. He was overcome and couldn't speak. Beatrice stopped.

"Please do it some more Persephone! You know, this is my first time."

"I thought so! Let me finish you off."

Beatrice straddled him and shoved his still-hard cock into her wet pussy. He didn't really arouse her, but it had been a long time since the last male, and she needed to get off. The heroin only provided half the solution. After several eternities, she felt his penis throb and a trickle of sperm dribble out of her cunt. The stream glowed red and purple. She pulled herself off him and collapsed on the bed. As her eyelids drooped, she could see the mourning dove hanging from the fluorescent overhead and she could feel a mix of panic and sadness overwhelm her. She closed her eyes and started to cry softly.

Darkness came home in a gray cloud which morphed into blackness as she counted the ticking clocks.

She awoke very slowly; lead was flowing through her brain — thoughts were frozen. She heard a familiar cooing sound. The mourning dove was making its signature sounds. She was still wearing her girlfriend's boots. they made her feel safe. Beatrice relished the leather protection. Her pussy was sticky and sore and she had an iron taste in her mouth. Her hands were trembling. Some sunlight was filtered through the dirty window. She glanced at the clock on the wall, it was 3:00. Must be 3 p.m. How long?

To steady herself she reached out, expecting to grab a part of Alessandro's body. Her fingers touched wetness, sticky and warm and thick. She got up and saw that she was lying next to a pool of red. She was frightened and yet slightly thrilled by the crimson Rorschach on the white sheets. Danger was present — the mourning dove knew and the troll doll, who decided to make a brief appearance, smiled and acknowledged her sensations.

Beatrice eyes focused on the figure that had been staring at her for a very long time. It was about 6 feet tall; a torso clad in shadows of black leather. Hands clad in black leather gloves. The face was obscured by a single woman's stocking that had been stretched over its head and knotted on top: eyes and lips stretched beyond recognition. Once it knew it was noticed it left quickly through the door, something clattered on the floor.

Beatrice got up and walked unsteadily to where the figure had been standing. Now her brain acknowledged certain things. First that the figure had dropped a blood-stained straight razor with a mother of pearl handle. Second, her one-night stand, her lover, her toy, Alessandro from the night before, had been murdered. It was beyond murder and now that she was near the body, the smell of blood and urine made her gag. She knew something was wrong when she awoke but had refused to accept it. She swayed slightly in her boots and reached out to steady herself against the wall behind the corpse.

Her lover had been turned into a piece of meat. He was propped up against the wall, sitting in a pool of gore that had finally stopped spreading. The coagulation shimmered in the dim fluorescent light like an unholy sacrament. The sight simultaneously horrified and fascinated her. She couldn't avert her eyes, she was frozen in place and fighting back a gag reflex. At this time, she started remembering Criselda. It was curious that Beatrice hadn't thought of her for the past 24 hours. Now she was stuck with hallucinations, memories of her female lover and a corpse that was quickly growing rancid. She wanted to taste and smell Criselda again. Now it was possible that she might never see her friend again.

So Sweet, So Perverse, So Enchanting

Beatrice surveyed the corpse and the damage done. Both of Alessandro's ears had been removed, cropped very closely. All his fingers were lopped off. The ears and fingers were in a neat pile on his left. His arms (still attached) were at his sides. His pants had been pulled down, but not removed. His penis had been removed — a jagged cut that was now clotted. The penis had been shoved into Alessandro's mouth. Under each eye were marks reminiscent of Harlequin. The eyes had been gouged out — two blank sockets stared at her. A black dove was perched on each shoulder.

Beatrice slowly made her way to the closet and opened the door, which creaked and frightened her. She was shivering. Warmth. She found her black vinyl trench coat and put it on. She felt slightly better as she clutched the coat around her, so tightly that her dark red nails almost ripped the material. She had a bad case of the Scaries.

She then moved towards the front door, opened it just enough for her to slip out, and walked down the hall; the click clack of her heels echoed. There was a vacant apartment at the end of the hall. Beatrice entered and checked to make sure nothing was there. Just a void to keep her safe. It was empty and safe. She closed the door behind her, locked it and put the security chain.

She surveyed the area: the space was old and the plaster ceiling, which had been painted black, was populated with white hairline cracks reminding her of her mother's hair. The walls of the room were crimson and curved, imparting a gallery feel to the environment. She pulled the light cord and after a second or two the fluorescent overhead buzzed and came to life. The overhead light was one of those old circular tube jobs that caused all objects to display corrupted shadows.

Hemispheres of pain. Time was slippery and her brain split

into two perfect halves — disjointed in the extreme, they would never fit together again. That figure was coming back, it was certain. She realized she smelled of sex, her vagina was sore, and her muscles felt feverish. Flu-like aches. Clutching the trench coat tighter, she prayed to herself, then laughed. She was remembering Alessandro's corpse. It reminded her of things she did in the past. Murder used to please her, but now it made her ill, but she still got the joke. Beatrice wasn't sure anymore.

Beatrice slowly knelt, her leather boots creaking slightly. When she was in the prayer position, she wept. She remained there for an hour or so, staring at the intricate white spiderweb of the ceiling which appeared to be approaching. Just like her *nonna*. The hands reached out and she got closer to the floor, which was comprised of stained wood slats.

"God help me please." Random sounds of cooing birds and squeaky scratchy sounds of claws of beasts, crucified after their truncated lives. She had lost her rosary somewhere; she longed for it now.

Trying to stave off the fears and the yen for more chemical soothing. Silence was craved. "Why am I here again?"

Andromeda spoke to her. They hadn't communicated for a long time. The troll doll was hiding in the corner. Beatrice wanted to hear about the toy store. She longed to see Aurora again, to smell her hair and the back of her neck.

The troll smiled at her slyly, gave her a wink, then started to walk towards her. She was curious. Did it have the lucky horseshoe branded on the sole of its foot?

Her namesake Beatrice Cenci always told her to be wary of fathers, mothers, and lovers. The two of them would walk across the bridge sometimes in the August evenings discussing pain and loss. Her lovers carried the head which was dripping blood on a broken path. Crimson footsteps marked their journey from there to here. What was the fuckin' point? Beatrice fondled her knives and razors, enjoying the coldness. She licked one switchblade and enjoyed the taste and aroma of steel.

She always inhabited a dead-end street. At the end of the decayed road, the neighbors had been murdered. The radios had died. The old tube televisions had died from loneliness. A silence always cloaked her, becoming her legal guardian. Clad in lurid red and yellow, glowing and dancing with the beast of the yellow night. She grabbed the creature, licked its gums and stuck her tongue way down its throat. The creature panted and responded in kind.

The troll doll knew these things, but it told the women nothing.

They were in the city now. It had recently rained — wetness under their shoes, mixed with broken glass and gravel. Aroma of water, trash, and a little blood. They were invigorated by the new sensations which gave way to the Scaries. The Scaries — the impetus for their pain and destruction, the motivation for a quest for new skin. Hide with the other creatures in the abandoned house, make arrangements for annihilating the citizens and the politicians. A master plan for Zero.

Beatrice remembered the house — her parents' house, down the block from the toy store. A row house — her parents kept it in excellent condition, built in 1907. She had lived alone there her entire childhood until she ran away, bringing the images with her. Those things never left.

In Springtime:

The Cenci sat on the floor of the toy store, her back against the wall, next to the big window that she loved, the one whose shelf was loaded with antique toys thrown haphazardly in a pile. The linoleum under her legs was cool, soothing her sore muscles, The tiny blonde troll was perched on top of the toy pile watching with cold detachment. She couldn't decipher the words or the actions of the flurry of figures — a demonic kaleidoscope — moving around her and inside her. Aurora was gleefully maniacal with hysterical laughter in the extreme as she clutched an antique straight razor in her bloodstained left hand. Blood flecked her checks. She gave the blade a quick sexy lick.

"Where, I ask you? Where will she be?"

Time was moving slowly, and Beatrice could feel hands clawing at her as she watched Aurora slowly slice open the woman's throat. She could hear the metal slicing flesh — slow blood drain-gurgling iridescent. Beatrice merged her past thoughts to what she was viewing now. At each slash, Beatrice pushed herself against the wall. Flinching, crying.

Nowhere else. Aurora walked over and handed the razor to Beatrice.

"It's your turn now my pretty-pretty."

Beatrice took the instrument, walked over to the still writhing body and realized it was her mother. She knelt down next to the carcass and ripped open the white crimson-drenched blouse, she dragged the blade down the stomach, up and around, down and about, sideways to and fro, until she had created her own private sigil of protection. She would be safe now. Beatrice felt her eyes roll upwards, whiteness approaching, her ego dying, a cold rush of fluctuating darkness. The last sound she could recognize was Aurora's sultry voice.

"Sleep now, my pretty-pretty."

A cold palm soothed her brow.

When Beatrice regained consciousness in the toy shop many years ago, there was no one left except the toys — just the discarded broken dolls and miscellaneous playthings. The sinister troll had vanished. She realized she was clutching a soiled porcelain doll reminiscent of the Victorian era. Beatrice looked at the doll, studied the albino face — the cracked paint, the glass eyes — and kissed it gently on the lips. The fluorescent light had turned shades of deep blue.

Dia de los Muertos — complete fear. She knew the taste. It lingered on her tongue many times, caught in the back of her throat. It's the odor that tantalized her olfactory nerves. Tickle-tickle. She lived underneath grim clouds during this time and sleep was gone. A troll fondled her and spoke about things. It knew what had occurred. Sick whisperings invaded her bedroom each day at 4 a.m.

"I know you. I saw you. Dirty-dirty deep down inside. Taste it. Taste it. Ladies and gentlemen welcome to violence: the word and the act."

The stuff of evil — flexible demons combed her luxurious ebony hair, purging the pain as she did her makeup again. Sitting at her favorite vanity. A short timeout in the Sadistic Electric Spa. Special discounts. She counted her sins on her trembling digits. One, two, three. Time to replenish the juices.

"Malocchio!"

The woman counted out seven tarot cards, major arcana only, drew La Papesse and gently placed it on the vanity table. She continued doing her eye makeup, studying her actions in the hazed antique mirror. She shifted her position — leaned slightly left. The light was too bright. She got up and retrieved her favorite red scarf from her purse on the settee. She covered the gooseneck lamp attached to the mirror with the fabric. The effect of the crimson light amused her, but she soon removed it because she wanted her makeup to be accurate. It had to be the Apex of fashion; the others must drool with lust. The eyes were the most critical. Each eyelid was to have gradations of black, gray and purple. Extra mascara was required, and two sets of false eyelashes were essential for each eyelid. When the work was completed, she leaned in to admire the masterpiece. Her black hair reached her shoulders. The bangs ended just at the eyebrows. The eyelids began with a shade of black on top, gradually morphing into purple by the lashes. She fluttered her eyelids and nodded approval.

"The colors compliment my ebony Sicilian eyes."

She never wore lipstick because she didn't want to detract from her eyes, besides, her lips were full and naturally rosy, didn't need any assistance.

It was getting late, the stage needed her, and she lusted for the stage.

Lights flashed three times quickly in the room: brief highlights of wandering shadows previously captured by the Ouija board — now traveling, gently caressing her. The female form they had waited for. She could smell the sweat and smoke of the spectators. Aurora would be so proud of her. They quickly became enamored of her taste — she reveled in their movements deep inside her. A cream, then a caress.

The assassins were here at last. She rolled onto her back, she was clad only in her corset — red and black jacquard satin under blue and red lights. Naked she strangled Mars and spread her legs wider. The music grew louder as unseen fleshy things entered her silence.

"Must keep quiet now. Play passive. Eventually everyone will leave."

She remained in a translucent pool, shimmering in the red beams. Naked now, she sighed.

"You don't know the truth I possess."

"This virus will hang over us until we stop."

Criselda had become an erotic contraption.

After her strip dance and flashes of sin, the ecdysiast left the stage amid the aroma of flesh and cum, alcohol and blood. The familiar mourning sounds began once more.

After a long while (she sensed) she came to in the room. Still fuzzy, she stood up and walked to the full-length mirror. It was very old, slightly cracked, sympathetic with her mind. She had the motive now and she would set the gears in motion.

"The hypothesis still remains — we're in the wrong place."

"Any one of us could be the killer."

"She was careless with her pussy, her pornographic life that she savored daily — a Klieg-light Klimax. Her fans are rabid things."

Watching, watching, watching inside a storm. Stacked heels — flash blood — stained black patent leather, she touched a spot rubbing the red color between her thumb and index finger. Gave it a taste.

"Salty. Sex of the witch — like all the other times?"

Talons in a circle — each occupied by a fractured mannequin. No words yet. She knew they spoke behind her back. Strange tastes.

"And these murders were just a smokescreen to hide our hatred for ourselves. So now we have nothing."

The hypodermic was filled with the fluid filtered through some cotton and hair, inserted and pulled back. Boot. Re-boot until the blood blossom that she loved appeared. She didn't resist.

"I know it won't kill me."

A random hand, drugged fingers wearing Javanese nails — cold silver — dragged across the albino flesh. A faint trail of red was drawn down her body, starting from under the chin and ending at the pubic bone. Writhing, pleasuring, finally withering, her moans were apparent, and the spectators craved more excitement. Captured on film. her cunt was wet and glowing, promising redemption.

The syringe, now empty, fell to the floor.

She fucked in a macabre cinema, known only to a few, next to the toyshop; a baptism. The loneliness of her evil comforted her. Criselda cradled Beatrice in her arms. They slept on the couch in front of the broken television. The blonde-haired troll was next to the hypodermic. Criselda's heartache kept her from sleeping comfortably, the iron taste in her mouth terrified her. At 3 a.m. thoughts of her losses awoke her. A music box, another toy a tune of reverie, a million dead clocks. They were paralyzed.

The People Downstairs Door Do Wicked Things

The moon was up and full and starting to shed red tears, which turned phosphorescent as they entered Beatrice's blood stream. These tears kissed her red blood cells, strengthening her lust and her obscene cravings. Soon, her mouth tasted of iron and her eyes became the color of film negative. It was the best moon for Halloween.

She sat by the window that was slightly open, breathing in the October air which was still warm but carried the smell of decay. She looked at her fingers. She could still make out the pale skin on her left ring finger where her wedding ring used to be. No more.

"I'm gone. Can't come back."

The naughty spot. That's what Beatrice craved. Just something to get her higher. She had just moved to the neighborhood, having recently relocated from the suburbs, a rather fast exit. She knew this place was a dump, but she was finally away, nestled in shadows of seclusion, surrounded by vibrating noise — a low hum that always lay under her thoughts. Thoughts that were often evil in nature. Beatrice loved her new apartment — it was across the street from the boardwalk — smells of danger and rot caressed her senses, begging her to partake, mixing with the sounds of the wooden rollercoaster and the odor of hotdogs and blood.

She hadn't finished furnishing it yet, just a small antique wooden table, a wooden chair. Both had been purchased from the junk store down the block, next to the carousel. Bare walls, bare bulb overhead.

The sex shop around the corner had piqued her curiosity. She had passed it last night on her way back from the storefront

Chinese restaurant, but she doubted she would ever pay it a visit; those places were pretty dull: bootleg DVDs and lame sex toys. The patrons were usually either smelly and old or perverted younger men — all sweaty; sweaty and sad. Stink of semen and sweat. They were the lost tribe of disastrous desires hiding in video booths while they discharged and wept. Beatrice didn't understand why she was remembering this now.

"But it's the best moon for Halloween."

Vacant eyes. She sat on the window ledge letting the warm autumn air slowly climb up her legs, invading the black triangle under her black leather mini skirt. With the fingers of her left hand she massaged herself. Afterwards she held her hand up for inspection, taking note of the fluid clinging to her fingers.

It was approximately 8 p.m. There were no trick-or-treaters in this neighborhood. The amusement park was still open. Today was the last day of the season. Open until midnight, then not again until the spring. Open Easter Sunday. Closing on Halloween.

Beatrice sang a gentle song to the item at her feet: a few days ago, she had decapitated her husband's head and placed it in a Plexiglas cube. Hermetically sealed. No chance of decay. After eating his heart, gobbling it up with glee, she had sawn off the head in hubby's basement workshop. Some of the blood and flesh had been consumed also, but not by her. That was the deed of her friends, the followers of the Black Science. It was their trademark. His eyes were sewn shut. Her wedding ring was sewn inside his mouth.

"You look good," Beatrice said.

He didn't answer. She held the box up to her face and gave the box a slight lick with her tongue, leaving a saliva mark which looked elegant in the moonlight that was creeping into her room. A slight pang of sadness, but Beatrice's electric disease squelched down any regret. A soft sucking sound could be faintly heard.

"No. Not here."

"I don't know why this happened, but I'm glad it did. The cops must have been curious, just before they ejaculated in unison, I really put them into an arousal fugue state. I just adore being the center of attention. Dead men tell no tales, neither do well fucked dead cops."

Beatrice placed the cube on the windowsill.

"The sea air has many health benefits.'

Distant distant slowly through my veins watch her work at it but no relief cobblestone memories I can't recapture unable to leave the basement, a collection of things waits for me inside wait for time wait for the previous slave.

I knew I was it. I was toxic for time the door swung open and I stabbed blindly eradicating arousal.

She lit a cigarette and exhaled smoke out the window. She thought of how she would entertain herself for the rest of the evening. After all, it was Halloween. She pulled open the table drawer and withdrew a glassine packet, rubber-stamped with the words *Black Sunday*, along with a spoon and an insulin hypo. Beatrice didn't remember the dealer who had given her the packet. It was rumored to feel like a mixture of crank and junk. She poured the contents into a spoon, added a few drops of water from the glass of water she had left on the table earlier, and heated the spoon briefly over a match flame. When she shot up, her head bolted back and her clitoris spasmed. Plasma juice shot into her cervix. Waves of languor fucked by friction and energy rushed through her body. Beatrice's skin suffered a cold burn. The burn subsided after a few minutes and she felt complete. A quick bolt of vomit shot out her mouth and landed on the floor. Very clean. No mess on her or her outfit.

when done I stuttered backwards talking teetered and sat down to watch the fungi colonize then I ravished then I punished "please wait" roughly tilted emotion-motion my mind is quite funny. quite funny. those chemicals. because post-mortem deterioration had forced a climax too soon upon a cross. an autopsy was really hurting let's attend to important business because of a death, cleopatra arrived she was so much braver than they were

Beatrice pulled on her engineer boots, opened her compact mirror and admired her shoulder-length black hair, her bangs which rested on her eyebrows. As she pulled on her black turtleneck, she heard undecipherable murmurs. She decided to wear her motorcycle jacket since it might get chilly later in the evening. Bidding her spouse goodbye, she walked out the room, down one flight of stairs and out to the street.

"Good evening, naughty boys and girls!"

Turning left, she rounded a corner and looked down the street to get her bearings. The street was barely illuminated by three antique streetlamps. At the end of the street was the sex shop she had noticed earlier. Beatrice made the decision to go pay it a visit, since she really had nothing else to do and the drug was making her twitchy and feisty.

The street smelled strongly of urine and something else she couldn't comprehend. As Beatrice continued to stroll, the mystery odor ate at her.

"Aaaaaaiiiiiieeeee, fuck!"

She turned around quickly when she heard the guttural wail off to the side; in a barely lit building entrance two figures appeared to be grappling. As Beatrice approached the two silhouettes the image came into focus, the film stuttered and burned. Two females held each other tightly, one had just gouged out the eye of the other and thrown the orb to the ground. The disembodied eye stared up at Beatrice from the sidewalk. Beatrice picked it up and handed it back to her owner, who was still screaming in pain.

"You're welcome."

Beatrice continued on her trip, which ended when she stopped at the entrance to the sex shop. The display window contained two mannequins that were dressed as naughty French maids, their bulbous plaster udders barely contained by their outfits. The floor was littered with sex toys and assorted sex paraphernalia. Beatrice entered.

Criselda was sitting behind a display case which served as a table for a cash register. The cash register was antique, inherited from her father who had opened a bodega at the same location for many years. He was gone now. The sex shop barely made money, but it served other purposes and she liked being the sole proprietor. She had just opened a book and started to read when she heard the door alarm go off. Beatrice's form slinked into view in the security mirror overhead. Criselda's fingers trembled and her mouth went dry.

"Hi I'm Criselda. Whatcha need?"

"Just looking." Beatrice turned and looked directly at Criselda.

"I like your sweater, " Beatrice said. "Mohair?"

"Yes. I always wear it when I wear leather pants."

Criselda got up from behind the display case. She walked over.

Criselda looked up and down at Beatrice, her ebony eyes drinking her up. She took Beatrice's left hand and looked it over.

"I see a ring is gone," she said as she slightly caressed Beatrice's ring finger. "Was it your choice?"

"That's a good way to put it."

As she said this, Beatrice felt a little tingle in her crotch. The moist breath and smell of Criselda made her a little dizzy.

"Don't be so nervous. I'm not going to do anything. I'm not going to hurt you."

Criselda grabbed Beatrice's left hand, taking it and placing it down the front of her leather pants, on top of her crotch. Beatrice's fingers parted the lips. She detected that Criselda was wet but there was something pearly hard between the lips of her cunt. Beatrice withdrew her hand and smelled her fingers. The smell on her digits was a combination of vaginal liquid and saliva. She placed her hand down the front of Criselda's pants again and decided to explore.

"In case you were wondering, it's teeth."

"What?" Beatrice asked.

"It's teeth, vulva dentata, it runs in my family. I have it. My mother has it. My sisters, my grandmother and aunts in Rome had it. "

Beatrice just stared at her. After a few seconds She tasted her fingers. Her new acquaintance smiled.

Criselda looked at Beatrice's eyes, then she pulled up Beatrice's sleeves, exposing the track marks.

"I see, I see..." Criselda smiled.

Beatrice tensed up, then said, "Why is the display case dark? Did the light blow out?"

"What? I didn't realize..." Criselda went back behind the case and switched on the light. Beatrice sucked in her breath as the tableau came into view.

The decapitated head of a middle-aged man was propped up behind the glass, around it were scattered some bones and cat skulls. Towards the left was a crucifix and some dried-up flowers. The eyes were gone, the flesh was starting to shrivel. Three mice were wandering around sporting atomic smiles; they briefly glanced at the humans, then turned away.

"That's my dad," Criselda said. "We were just chatting when you came in. I made him die in the best way possible. I had to jump him one night, took him from behind. Got him on the floor, had my box-cutter, ripped him from ear to ear. I remember he heaved as I remained on top of him, then he collapsed flat to the floor. It was fuckin' amazing! Made my pussy twitch! For a long time I stared at the puddle of blood underneath him. Blood never looks the same in real life as it does on TV. After awhile I got a hacksaw from downstairs and removed his head. Had to wait awhile for the blood to drain out. Then I placed him in the case. Later on I added some decorations, as you can see in the case. Not sure what the mice are doing in there. That was a couple of Halloweens ago. It's been there ever since."

At this moment, the door alarm went off again. They turned around and saw a middle-aged man in the store. He was perspiring. Criselda smiled.

"May I help you?"

"You got video booths here?"

"Yes, in the back. I'll show you."

"Wait. Wait. How much?" the patron said as he leered at the women. Beatrice felt more puke working its way back up, but another wave of the drug rush kicked in and the urge went away. She felt as if her eyes were on fire.

"Since it's Halloween, the first 10 minutes are free!"

The happy patron smiled. "Where is it?"

"In the back, I'll take you there."

She left Beatrice standing there as she walked the man to the back of the store, past the racks of slutty lingerie, leather, gear, sex toys, and bondage equipment.

Beatrice watched as they disappeared behind a red velvet curtain. She heard a door open and Criselda's words fading: "It's right down the stairs." A few minutes later Beatrice's ears were enticed by the low sounds of moaning and screaming. Infernal soundtracks for her pleasure.

After about ten minutes Criselda re-emerged alone. "He's down there enjoying himself." Criselda smiled.

"Oh! How many booths are down there?"

"Twelve."

"Want to see? We'll bring the next one down together."

"I'd love to."

walk down down down watch the victims squirm taste burnt metal skin smooth trapped sweaty fur and leather in the October sticky rain she's reaching toward the shiny things and stops just before the monster beyond the stars as told by the people below the ground look down fuzz fall fuck

The door alarm sounded once more. Both women turned around quickly and stared at the thirty-ish male who had just come in. He was in a business suit. He also inquired about the peep booths.

"Sure we have 'em, signore," Beatrice said. "I'm Beatrice, this is Criselda, we'll take you downstairs and show you. We have quite a nice setup. Don't we?"

Criselda was slightly taken aback by Beatrice's sudden assertiveness but nodded in agreement.

"Nice suit! You a salesman?" Beatrice continued.

"No, not at all. I'm a trader," he said indignantly.

"Oh! Sorry about that!" Beatrice apologized, "Sure, let's go downstairs. This way behind the curtain. By the way, in honor of Halloween, the first ten minutes are free! Criselda, please lead the way!"

Beatrice escorted the gentleman, taking his arm as they followed Criselda behind the curtain and down the stairs. Beatrice noticed that his eyes were riveted on Criselda's ass, tight in the black leather pants. There was a smell of mildew and that unknown odor that Beatrice had detected on the street. At the bottom of the stairs was a decrepit door that was covered with cracked red paint. Criselda opened the door and they stepped in. The room was dark except for a row of 12 peep booths. Each booth was identified by a neon number.

"Let's all go into booth 3, it's big, it'll fit all of us," Criselda said. The man eagerly walked ahead toward the third booth.

Criselda led them to booth 3, opened the door and they all stepped in. The light came on. The booth contained three stools. Criselda had the man sit on the middle stool and Beatrice and her on either side. Criselda put a red token into the slot and the black barrier lifted in front, exposing a window 2 feet by 2 feet wide. Criselda grabbed the man by the neck and pressed his face against the glass.

"Take a look, baby!"

Beatrice also looked and what she saw excited her immensely. There was a circular red stage lit by one floodlight. Under the light was the patron Criselda had led down earlier. He was naked and tied to a chair, blood poured out of his mouth painting his naked chest. He was moaning and weeping. His penis was erect because someone had fastened a cock ring around it. Strips of skin had been removed from his chest. His tears were plentiful. His feet were fastened to the floor with long nails. Two women, naked, were on their knees on either side of him, drinking from deep gouges in each wrist. He twitched every so often.

"Those are my babies," Criselda said. "See how beautiful they are? My daddy didn't like them! So sad! See his mouth? His tongue is gone, he tried to eat me out. Shit, was he surprised when my cunt ripped his tongue out!"

"I thought we were going to watch porn! Not a haunted house!" the man complained. "What is this Halloween shit? You dumb cunts! This shit don't even look real! I'm getting the fuck out of here! Fucking skanks!"

"Wait, wait, signore. Don't get angry," said Criselda.

"Fuck you, foreigner!"

When she heard the insult, Beatrice's anger kicked in, fueled by Black Sunday.

"Hold on, baby! Calm down! You're making me so hot!" Beatrice purred.

Beatrice winked and moved in as if to kiss him. He calmed down and smiled. He took her lead and leaned in for an intimate moment. Beatrice took his top lip in her mouth lovingly, bit down hard, and ripped it clean off his face, sending blood flying over the window, the booth, and her and

Criselda. His screams only increased her anger and frenzy and the wetness between her legs. Criselda caught the fever also and ripped his ear off, spitting it onto the floor.

"It's real padre, it's real... It's real just like your eye that I'm gouging out!" His shrieks grew very loud and vomit was coming out of his mouth. A soft rip-squish and the orb was free. Criselda showed him the eye in her hand — a lump of flesh and a couple of veins perched in her hand, dripping goo to the floor of the booth. Sister Streetfighter.

"Here! Look at it with your last fuckin' good eye. Stronzo."

The man slumped over onto the floor.

"That was fun," said Criselda.

"I think he passed out," said Beatrice.

"Good. Pull his pants down, get him hard."

Beatrice did as she was told and when he was erect, Criselda, pulled her pants down, exposing her vulva, which was moaning. She sat down on top of his cock and when it was fully in, bore down. Beatrice heard a soft ripping of flesh and she noticed a flood of blood gushing out from beneath Criselda, who was oblivious, her neck bent back, eyes rolling up, tears exuding from the corners of her eyes.

Criselda spoke in tongues as her climax waned.

"Fuck! Fuck! I needed that!"

When done, Criselda dismounted and pulled her pants up.

"Come on, cutie. Let's drag him out to the stage. I'll tell the girls to get another chair. Business should be booming tonight. Come on. I'll introduce you to my girls. I think you'll like them. They don't talk very much though. Ooof! He's heavy.

Businessman asshole! Cheap cocksucker! I'll get some mops and Clorox — we have to clean this shit up. I have a feeling we'll be busy tonight."

It was now 4 a.m.

Beatrice and Criselda surveyed the peep show area under the sex shop. There were 7 males ranging in age from thirties to seventies, each tied to a chair, each drained of blood, each mauled beyond recognition. Criselda's two daughters lay curled up in fetal positions, sleeping on the floor, sated and content, enjoying sweet dreams of torture and bliss. Beatrice was coming down from her drug high, slight depression was kicking in, the night's activities a soft slow blur that she would always remember. Her mouth tasted like iron.

"We'll clean this up later. No one is going anywhere. The girls need their rest. Let's close up and go to the beach," Criselda said.

"Listen, I have to clean up," Beatrice said, "We're covered in blood, semen and who knows what other shit. I don't have a change of clothes."

"I'll take care of that. I live above the shop. Let's go."

The women went upstairs. After Criselda locked the shop door from the inside, they went up a hidden staircase to Criselda's apartment. Beatrice liked the apartment: it was a hybrid of Victorian splendor and early seventies décor. Not exactly the stuff of suburban dreams, but it worked and somehow it made Beatrice comfortable.

"You know," Criselda said, "I'm alone here. The girls have their own room to stay in. If you have no place to go you can stay with us. There's an extra room, you can furnish it any way you want."

"I'll think about it. Do you have any clothes I can borrow?"

"Sure. After we're cleaned up and dressed do you want to go to the beach? The sun will rise soon. Plus, the beach is officially closed now, so there will be no city officials bothering us."

"Sure. That would be nice."

Later the two new friends sat on the beach very close to each other. They were wearing identical white lace dresses. Beatrice's head lay on Criselda's shoulders. The sun was just starting to peek up. Beatrice had enjoyed getting dressed with Criselda.

watching seagulls wet females laughing children with their families dads looking down white lace remember her white lace hold this thought forever white garter belt black lacquered toenails translucent glowing droplets of blood on the upper thigh teeth glow glow glow don't leave the shadow people will come back

For the first time in a very long while, Beatrice was at peace. Revenge was complete.

"Criselda?"

"Yes?"

"Next season, when the rides are open again, can we ride the Carousel?"

If only it could be that way.

The Lustful Touch of Scorned Lovers

Air and fire bathed her figure of darkness while twisted angels licked her clean.

"How do you know my name?" Beatrice asked. Things were distant now.

Lips touched gently on pale clammy flesh; her mouth wanting to eat the flesh it caressed. Rules were eradicated and she whimpered as her breath quickened. More assassins had arrived, urging her to one climax after another. She relished the feeling of being filled and re-filled time after time. The sounds of dead cocks comforted her. As the rabid phalluses penetrated, as her labia gripped tightly, as Criselda watched in fear, teeth nibbled on her neck. She was already martyred by a tongue of guilt.

Quiver, quiver in the dark — a new pleasure previously hidden exposed her mortal sin on the electric altar of altered states. Semen crawled down the wall, anthropomorphic slight feeding frenzy. Criselda had lost the ability of speech as she was devoured by the white light of the murders that had occurred. She had been unable to prevent anything. In her apartment now, she had given up control. A symphony of twisted digits spread her vaginal walls as she hummed an arcane tune that she remembered from childhood. Her blood-spattered breasts had become a new expression.

Pain at the blood chateau, hiding behind the sounds of rapid flicking tongues. Hiding from the shadows of the rabid punk kids hanging out around the corner, smoldering in the moist evening heat. It was near the five and ten shop several blocks away. Criselda and Beatrice the Cenci disappeared again under the Rabid Moon.

Beatrice touched her friend's black hair then leaned forward and buried her face in the luxuriant strands. She craved the aroma and she needed nourishment.

"The pain keeps me whole; it completes me. A new aura around my being."

She continued fondling Criselda's locks. After several minutes, Criselda gently pulled away, took Beatrice's hands in hers and gently kissed each finger. She could feel the virus of The Cenci taking hold; its grip was tightening and Criselda was frightened.

Television paranoia. Clouds of obscure pain. The most popular snack in the country.

"Are you sure?"

Electric, naked on the altar. Criselda's spasm intertwined with that of Beatrice. The fluid acted like some sort of drug, an electric opioid Aktion of unknown cause. Blackness tinged with purple enveloped them.

Criselda had familiarized herself with the sexual rituals, obliterating those who tried to remove their pleasures. Tired. So tired. A spectral creature touched her. The Cenci began to speak of the Lost Saints while fantasizing about the dive bar where she would pluck victims from the drunken patrons to use for her dalliances. Speakers blasted scratchy rock n' roll as her eyes teared. Wax figures burned outside the leather windows; lost widows chanted softly, happy to be rid of their spouses.

A building crumbled behind them, the dirt coated their black corsets, drawn tightly so the restraint would accentuate their climaxes. In a daze, Criselda's thoughts began to wander aimlessly.

"I want to feel content free from nerves. Following me day by day, night by night. Postmortem insignificance."

"I'll go and hide again when I sleep, far away from the Scaries."

A dark blue oblong box captured Beatrice's facial expressions; cars drove by the abandoned road. No one sees them anymore. She brought them there for a fuck and some pain. She searched through the myriad of dots until she located her own face. Cold shakes. In the hallway, things shifted, and their mouths kissed. Lips touched their labia. Moving slowly, her limbs were becoming numb.

The sea air of Ostia was wrapped in electric stains, remembering guilt and Pasolini, tempting her nostrils and exciting her salivary glands. The Lunar Moths glowed at 3 a.m. She carried a crescent moonbeam between her thighs. The smell of sweat, spunk and assassination hung in the air. A cracked TV screen replayed key episodes from her life: 5 feet 5 inches, slim, buxom bound in wet leather poured into a stylish outfit, sleek as a laser, strolling through the arcades. A pickup, she will be there on time. Every 20 feet or so, a camera snaps a photo, another entry for the morgue gallery. Laying plans for future victims. A knife penetrates bare flesh, slowly slicing open the cellular structure. This evening is punctuated with low silent screams.

Criselda tasted the blood — she craved it now and she couldn't exist without it. The viral infection in her brain was taking root. She donned the black leather gloves once more and proceeded to eviscerate the male before her.

"No. No. I have a family. I..."

She silenced him with a slash to the throat. She smiled as his expression betrayed a surprise and he slumped to the ground with a soft thud. Kneeling next to him, she reveled in the sound of gurgling blood, laughing at the final twitch of the death nerve.

All quiet now. She enjoyed prying open his mouth with the straight razor she clenched in her shaking left hand and inserted a blonde troll into his mouth.

"Such a pretty young man. Just out for a drink and a fuck. Such a little man. Never meant to live this long. What's happened to you?

She caressed the scent of death in her brain, twisted and burnt. Soft things. A ticking timepiece. A door opened. Images of loss and longing to see and in the distance, Beatrice laughed with relief. Everyone was watching and no one was watching.

"Sally go round the roses. Sally go round the pretty roses."

She was humming now — a staccato voice embellished the evening and the ocean was nearby. There was cooing and sea waves.

"You're my favorite sweetheart, you know that, right?" Far away far away moaning — tasty — tasty. An image too distant. A certain sacrifice. A crucified Barbie Doll under glass. A faint aroma of hydrochloric acid: the stuff that dreams are made of; the stuff of her fractured vision. No comment was necessary. A scream and then a dense black wall. They were waiting for the neon illumination over and over again. They never came. She is still waiting out there.

Slices of air. A body is motionless on the beach. The events that led up to the murder: a hole bored in the landscape, cracked windows, a sexual overdrive.

"I guess we'll burn in hell, now."

Illicit references to tunes without sound.

"I have feelings."

Plastic screams mis-remembered. Cold lips on warm glass. provocative protractions of ingenues in a chorus, castrated lechers that made the women ill and angry. Criselda and

154

Beatrice were wild creatures caught with the neutron bomb in their cervix, sucking in the ozone for a cheap high, selling tickets to the random-flesh-freak show.

"Please sing for me, Criselda."

"The curse that begins with a kiss..." was the reply.

A Technicolor Farewell from a Rabid Lover

Criselda awoke with brain and lips numb. Why?

The apartment was empty and had been so for two days.

It was 1 a.m. Criselda decided to read the note that Beatrice had mailed to her the day before.

"My love, my dear baby, I must leave you now. I've overstayed my welcome and the police will be searching for me. Those degenerates will never find me. How could they? If they find me, then they find you, my sweet girl. Wouldn't that be funny? Just look in the mirror sometime."

Criselda felt something tingling, warm on the back of her hands. She stopped reading for a moment and noticed that the backs of her hands were stained with splotches of pale red, causing her skin to itch. The splotches got darker, marking her Original Sin. Wouldn't the nuns be proud?

"It just makes it worse when you are that way, when the bloodlust drives you forward," the letter continued. "If there ever was love between us, I don't know. Maybe we'll talk in the future when things have calmed down. There have been many murders we have committed together. You don't remember them anymore, but I was there. They happened. Even when you were alone, I was there. The rabid pain eating away at our brains. I need these images again. To exist. To die. To love. I forgot where I should be or where I belong. It's not the way God wanted. It's 3 a.m. as I write — the creatures came to speak to me again about many things. *Adieu*, my broken doll, we'll never find all the pieces. We'll never fix it; perhaps in Aurora's toyshop."

There was a void surrounding the tableau. She felt a heartache for the first time.

Criselda smelled the paper, it had Beatrice's odor — moist and slightly bitter. She ripped the paper up with a vengeance and flung the pieces up in the air. Her tears were burning her cheeks. The confession and the realization etched lines of pain in her heart.

Criselda decided to go for a stroll even though it was very early in the morning. When she was outside, she walked slowly down the vacant streets. She hoped the sun would not rise. She hoped that the moon would remain forever. She suppressed a gasp as she stood in the piazza, looking upwards. It was a dense, heavy night; she could make out the outlines of eyes in the gathering clouds. She walked away with nothing as a gentle rain started.

She walked for an hour until she came upon a small bridge. Beatrice was waiting on the other side. They embraced and strolled together; their boots click-clacked on the wet pavement as they walked together into nighttime. Criselda fondled the stiletto in her left pocket. The knife was cold and comforting. Beatrice looked down at their feet and smiled.

They knew what had to be done.

Rome, Italy 2018 / New York City, USA 2019

Originally from Gravesend, Brooklyn, NYC, **Peter Marra** lived in the East Village from 1979 to 1993 at the height of the punk / no wave / art and music rebellion. He has had a lifelong fascination with Surrealism, Dadaism, and Symbolism; some of his favorite writers being Paul Eluard, Arthur Rimbaud, Tristan Tzara, Edgar Allan Poe, and Henry Miller. Peter also cites Roger Corman and Russ Meyer as influences.

His earliest recollection of the writing process is, as a 1st grader, creating a children's book with illustrations. The only memory he has of this project is a page that contained a crayon drawing of an airplane, caught in a storm. The caption read: "The people are on a plane. It is going to crash. They are very scared." His parents were always disturbed by that first book.

A Dadaist and a Surrealist, Peter's writings explore alienation, addiction, the function and misuse of love and attraction, the curse of secrets, the pain of victimization and the impact of multi-obsessions. He has had over 200 poems published either in print or online in over 25 journals.

His published works include ***approximate lovers (downtown materialaktion)*** from Bone Orchard Press, ***Vanished Faces (a performance of occult infections)*** from Writing Knights Press, and **Peep-O-Rama: Sins of the Go-Go Girls** & **Random Crucifixions: Obsessions, Dolls & Maniac Cameras** from Hammer & Anvil Books.

Peter was Danse Macabre's 2018 Artist-in-Residence.

Other titles in quality paperback from

HAMMER & ANVIL BOOKS

Fiction

Miles
Adam Henry Carrière

Described as, "a five-star bildungsroman with the emotional intensity of a symphony" every bit as intense and vivid as James Joyce's Araby, this tender, sweet tale nearly startles in the accuracy of its portrayal of emerging gay adolescence when such a thing was scarcely acknowledged much less discussed. Immersed in the words of Miles, the reader discovers a complexity of character with a level of introspection rarely found in such a visceral narrative. The writing is at once cerebral and highly emotive, set against a tapestry of sights and sounds that position the reader inside the main character's troubled, elegantly analytical mind. Characters large and small are complex, relatable, and drawn with remarkable authenticity; their dialogue makes you feel as if you're in the room with them. The story avoids the cliché of 'doubts' about identity and disaffected youth, while the self-assured narrative never fails to entertain. The pages fly by with one marvelous description after the next, reaching its zenith when describing the complex, often awkward, and unforgettable moments of attraction — the longing, excitement, and tenderness, as well as the loss and mourning — in this "strangely beautiful work of art."

Shant
Adam Henry Carrière

Behind Hollywood's tinsel curtain lies a web of crisscrossing shadows, where seemingly normal people living outwardly normal lives indulge their carnal hobbies and grab quick 'cups of coffee' amid the rubble of a condemned inner-city building stocked with bodies and addicts, quick buys and slow death. In this haunting saga, cul-de-sacs of 'normalcy' conceal pulsating sexual ghettos where hollow proprieties are defied, unforgiving avenues are escaped, admirable illegalities are executed, and luxuriant sensual awakenings are paid for — in blood. SHANT is a finely crafted voyage across the lives of discarded people whose ultimate redemption will fully engross readers of grandly told literary fiction.

Rowdies
J. Eric Castro

Every pastime has a beginning. Chock full of facts and folklore, legerdemain and legends, ROWDIES depicts professional baseball in its infancy. It is the story of Connie "Yank" Griffin, and out-of-work laborer who becomes a professional baseball player to feed his young family, and team manager G.E. Devlin, universally considered "The Greatest Man Ever to Grace the Diamond." Together and with the rest of their Nine, they take us on a journey through one season of late nineteenth century professional baseball — a world where beer sold by the quarter is drank by the gallon, where cheating ballplayers will do anything to win — or lose, and where an aging legend can ride the back of a desperate kid towards a final shot at glory in the twilight of his storied career. Fans of historical fiction and lovers of baseball alike will delight in this tale of balls... and strikes.

NEW! The Mooncalf and Other Tales
James Kendley

Celebrated author James Kendley presents for your literary degustation THE MOONCALF AND OTHER TALES, a storytelling buffet fit for the most discerning epicures of the macabre. This volume features a mouth-watering menu of occult subjects, supernatural happenings and visitants, each dish marinated in cauldrons of dark whimsy, modern horror, golden-age-style Weird Fiction, silver-age-style Science Fiction, as well as 'The Enthusiast,' a new novelette exclusive to this collection that returns to the forbidding worlds of Kendley's breakthrough novels The Devouring God & The Drowning God. In an era of rote, commodified fiction, THE MOONCALF AND OTHER TALES is a bracing aroma wafting with vivacity, a collection of gripping interest to gastronomes of hair-raising non-GMO anecdotes, coloratura vegan verse, and imaginative gluten-free feuilleton.

NEW! A Naked Kiss from a Broken Doll
Peter Marra

In the tradition of Italian film horror masters Mario Bava, Dario Argento and Sergio Martino, comes A NAKED KISS FROM A

BROKEN DOLL, the debut novel from acclaimed New York City poet Peter Marra. In this startling tale, two women are marked by Fate to plunge headlong into a psychotic netherworld, where broken dolls are rendered into lost souls by the three deadliest desires: Sex, addiction and murder. On every page, you will share the inner torments of original sin meticulously, deliciously wrought in glorious Eastmancolor. Rarely seen in contemporary storytelling, creatures from the underground take center stage bathed not in derision or loathing, but in humility and even love. A NAKED KISS FROM A BROKEN DOLL will haunt you from the first caress to long after the final climactic scream.

Jehrico: Many Tales of a Mexican Boy Making His Way in the Old West
Tom Sheehan

Introducing Jehrico Taxco — part-time businessman, hero junk collector, and leading citizen of the eponymous Bola City, in the wide-open American Southwest of old. In the grand tradition of the Western, Jehrico is a dubious hero, often uncertain of his correctness but blessed with a certain quiet goodness found throughout classic American storytelling. And like his literary forebears, Jehrico is as much a state of mind as a character. In JEHRICO, author Tom Sheehan brings the Western current, speaking to contemporary readers about surviving in a splintering culture and sustaining a secure community in both spirit and place, blending hitherto simple folk into courageous figures seeking lives of their own even while linking hands for the common good. Journey with JEHRICO into the warp and woof of the legendary American West, where pure storytelling magic unfolds.

Poetry

Faschingslieder
Adam Henry Carrière

This distinctive poetry collection ranges from short lyric pieces to extended narrative works with an array of recurrent themes such as physical and spiritual geographies; the weight of ancestry, culture, and dream worlds; the nexus between sensuality and sexuality; and mosaics of queer identity, real or perceived, false or profound, within a grasping society. And throughout, there is music — verbal, linguistic, and stylistic; the music of love, loss, and lust wrought through poetic rhythm, melody, and harmony which opulently adorn the carnivalesque pages of FASCHINGSLIEDER.

Rhododendrons of the Sea
Adam Henry Carrière

The centuries-long love affair between poetry and flowers endures in Adam Henry Carrière's RHODODENDRONS OF THE SEA. In this lush collection, oblong stages of life and fluid states of mind are fashioned into successions of lyrical portraits ala Baudelaire and Apollinaire, while rich Impressionistic landscapes are imbued with the authority and deep mystery of memory, color, and all the senses. Evocative and provocative in equal parts, electric as well as erotic, RHODODENDRONS is a coloratura poetic gallery that, long after the reading is done, will reverberate across the imagination of readers.

Peep-O-Rama: Sins of the Go-Go Girls
Peter Marra

On 7/31/2002 42nd Street, Times Square a.k.a. the "Deuce" heaved its final death rattle. As the New York Times reported: "The formal closing yesterday of the last peep palace on 42nd Street, Peep-O-Rama, was a coda in the rebirth of Times Square as a kinder, gentler place. The sex shops and naughty tape stores have been wiped clean from the famed street." This is the starting point for Peter Marra's landmark poetry collection PEEP-O-RAMA, where poems expose the inner workings of the psyche, a dissection of the state of America past and present, an exploration of love, alienation and addiction. Drop the tokens in the slot and wait for the curtain to rise on the tableau of the lost souls as they reach for the brass ring. This is a poetry collection for mature audiences you will not soon forget.

Random Crucifixions
Obsessions, Dolls & Maniac Cameras
Peter Marra

It's time to take a rollercoaster ride through the underbelly of the American landscape. RANDOM CRUCIFIXIONS, the shocking poetry collection from Peter Marra, depicts the bad, bare, and cruelly beautiful in the erotic nightscape of a decaying city. This oneiric haze of 58 poems offers up a narcotic cocktail of love often lost, love occasionally reclaimed, relationships shattered, and yes, the rare epiphany. Make the sign of the cross and pray for forgiveness amid the abandoned homes and decaying hotels of America as you ardently devour all the

RANDOM CRUCIFIXIONS...

NEW! **Hydrogen Sofi**
Tanya Rakh

Lose yourself in this dark, sensuous elegy to a hallucinogenic love —
manic, disorienting, and rife with blood and concrete. Through eight
prose-poem letters and an accompanying menagerie of freeform
surrealist poems, HYDROGEN SOFI is the breathtaking debut
collection of poetry from Tanya Rakh. Through her keen eye,
unrepentant ardor, and a startling sense of incorporeal consciousness,
HYDROGEN SOFI navigates the ecstasy, confusion, and grief of
surviving an ill-fated affair with a cruel, impossible muse. Hear
shadows laugh as they dance across the walls, just out of reach. Enter a
gray apartment filled with burning tapestries, the lovers aflame inside.
Pierce the flesh-red center of a series of poetic lies too beautiful to let
go.

The Jean Genie
Mercedes Webb-Pullman

Acclaimed New Zealand poet Mercedes Webb-Pullman's new collection
THE JEAN GENIE is a gorgeous and startling work, a collection of new
poetry influenced by and paying homage to Jean Genet. Ms. Pullman
paints portraits inspired by Genet's Our Lady of the Flowers, The
Miracle of the Rose, and The Thief's Journal, each of which are used as
a springboard for a descent into hell and an ascent into heaven,
captivating the reader through its eloquent, serene and tortured
palette. Her words are tactile and nimble, generating visions of sex, art,
sadistic beauty and scorched love, all couched in lyrical and rhythmic
patterns. Like Genet, Pullman's rich collection pushes the envelope to
create a treasure trove of poetic revelations for lovers of language and
image alike.

The Danse Macabre Anthologies

Amour Sombre

Romance darkly in AMOUR SOMBRE, the premiere print anthology
drawn from the archives of Danse Macabre ~ An Online Literary
Magazine™. Featuring a cornucopia of authors from around the world
and beyond the grave, AMOUR SOMBRE caresses readers with the
chill of ardour, the thrill of passion, and the poisonous pills of both the

melancholy and the macabrely. Here is a collection of dark delights for spirited spirits that will grip you like friendly (and perhaps not so friendly) shadows in the night.

Belles-lettres

BELLES-LETTRES is a bacchanalian celebration of the art of poetry, featuring over eighty authors from around the world and beyond the grave. Each unique piece seeks to kidnap the imagination of a reader, to plunge them on a trip that will electrify their perception of reality and accompany them from the forbidden shadows of feeling to the climax of wisdom's harsh sunlight. Whether strange or robust, enigmatic or thrilling, the cavalcade of mesmeric international voices will enthrall composers of poetry and keen readers of it alike. Bathe in the art of the mystic and re-arrange your poetic psyche now! Enter if you dare the aesthetic hive of the pathos found on every page of BELLES-LETTRES...

Goulash

A writer perpetually seeks the brother-bond, the club-house joy, the duet-voice of another soul searching for whole messages by the addition of one word at a time, a brick at a time in a wall at a time, looking for the lone or hidden word to complete the next text piece in line, hoping to find the same soul in another soul looking back at you, a mirror-host, a new voice in an old body, a replication whose thirst for words is endless, is the same as yours, or, indeed, surmounts it. This search for one word you hope is the perfect fit, fits the *goulash* that abounds for this use, the market, we dare agree, is huge, centuries in the making, lives in the making, books bound or loose for the fitting. Drawn from the locked coolers of issues lost to time, GOULASH is gourmet DM distilled, featuring an international buffet of tasty fictions and artisanal poetry... not to mention more than a few surprise ingredients readers worldwide have come to expect from DM for over a decade.

Hauptfriedhof

Gourmands of the fantastic, epicureans of the grotesque, and lovers of the furry, the freaky, and the far-out, we bid you welcome to HAUPTFRIEDHOF, the second print anthology drawn from l'ossuaire ancien du Danse Macabre! Over fifty-three works by a buffet of today's most irresistible storytellers are contained here. No author in this leviathan anthology is lonely for context or resonance, and each work, beautiful and engaging in itself, is amplified by its milieu... betwixt light and darkness. Danse Macabre believes in literature as spectra (not ghosts, but plural of spectrum) of history, of geography, of languages. Here, chilling circumstances, unsettling characters, exotic locales, often hilarious turns of the screw, and perhaps even a nightmare or two, abound. HAUPTFRIEDHOF is a lurid literary delight for aficionada of the monstrous — and monsters of all shapes and sizes!

Kismet

Picture yourself as an awkward child and recall that beautiful and terrible moment when you first were pulled in four directions by fear, fascination, disgust and longing. Whether it was in 1931 or yesterday, that moment whetted your appetite and, very, *very* sure your parents wouldn't approve, you wanted *more*. You were made for KISMET. Drawn from a treasure chest of lost DM issues, KISMET features a trove of bookish surprises from around the world and beyond the grave of the sort readers worldwide have delighted to in DM for over a decade. KISMET celebrates this shared joy in the unusual and the fantastic with this ample collection. Savor the delicious shivers traveling up and down the circuitry of your spine. Pierce the ominous mist and grab KISMET by the throat. Each entry in this anthology is a tidbit of uneasiness to be savored.

Weihnachtsmarkt

They say good things come to those who wait. Or almost die in the process, as the case may be. Truly, hunger is the savoriest of spices, and anticipation the greatest complement to pleasure. Drawn from the decorative pages of Danse Macabre ~ An Online Literary Magazine™ WEIHNACHTSMARKT is your supreme buffet of *feiertagsgeschichten* (holiday stories) et *poésie saisonnière* (seasonal poetry). Lovers of noir coloratura will groan under the weight of bookish delights from around the globe and beyond the grave, the finest fare on the literary web: prose plum puddings spiced with nutmeg and rum, hearty portions of DM's Prix de Noël winners topped with poetic sprigs of holly, hidden holiday crackers filled with mystery and caprice, flurries of powdered sugar, perhaps the faintest whiff of classical sulphur and that tang of bitter almond... ach du liebe, what a carve-up! Let no anthology reader in your macabrely circles go without WEIHNACHTSMARKT this holiday season!

are available exclusively on
Amazon.com
{US GB FR DE IT SP}

Interested in joining the H&A family of authors?
We seek progressive-alternative literary fiction
collections of short fiction & creative nonfiction
and adult-themed poetry

Inquire at
lazarusmediallc at gee mail dot com

Printed in Great Britain
by Amazon

11905032R00099